W9-ADV-507

↑

The Wild Birds

Six Stories

of the

Port William

Membership

WENDELL BERRY

NORTH POINT PRESS *San Francisco*

The author and publisher gratefully acknowledge *Mother Jones* magazine for prior publication of "Thicker Than Liquor" and "The Wild Birds."

North Point Press
850 Talbot Avenue
Berkeley, California
94706

For my sisters, Markie and Mary Jo

Contents

The Wild Birds

Thicker
Than
Liquor
(1930)

When the telephone rang, Wheeler Catlett was thinking about his future. Not that he knew much about it. The future was going to surprise him, as it had surprised all his mothers and fathers before him, but he had hopes. He had come back from his eastern law school four years ago, set himself up as a lawyer in two upstairs rooms overlooking the courthouse square in Hargrave, and increased his yearly income from nearly nothing to almost a living, with prospects for improvement. And now he was a married man with a future that needed thinking about.

Between his own hard times and those of the nation, Wheeler had grown familiar with the scarcity of money—indeed, as the son of a struggling small farmer, he had never known an abundance of it—and the present year of drouth and depression certainly offered no promise of financial astonishment. But he had worked hard, been careful, paid attention, lost no time, wasted nothing, and in spite of the hard times, he now and again had a few small bills to rub together. And that was partly what he was thinking about: the heartwarming friction of one piece of legal tender against another. These were not thoughts that could be considered mercenary; he had no yearning for mere money in a pile. He was thirty years old, he had been married just under a month, and money, for him, was as symbolic as it should be. His need for it tended as much toward substantiality as did his love for his bride. He was thinking about a home of his own, a place of his own. He liked his thoughts—which were, in fact, visions of Bess as happy as she deserved to be—and that was why he let the phone ring three times before he answered.

"I'm trying to get hold of Mr. Wheeler Catlett."

"This is Wheeler Catlett speaking."

"Mr. Catlett, this is the desk at the Stag Hotel in Louisville. We have a message for you from Mr. Leonidas Wheeler, who is staying here."

"Well, what's the message?"

"He says to tell you that he's sick, and he has no way to get home."

"Is he drunk?"

"I'm afraid so, sir. And, ah, his situation with respect to his bill appears to be somewhat embarrassing."

"I'll bet it is." Wheeler looked at his watch. "All right. I'll be there as soon as I can."

He hung up, and then rang and asked for his home number.

"Hello," Bess said.

"Would this be the beautiful young widder Catlett?"

"Herself. What did he die of?"

"Love, of course."

"For me?"

"For you."

"Well, wasn't that sweet!"

"Bess, my star client, Uncle Peach, requires my services at Louisville."

"Oh goodness! Is Uncle Peach having one of his attacks?"

"He's about worked his way down to the lower side of one, it sounds like. I don't know when I'll be home."

"I'll expect you when I see you?"

"I'm afraid so, Bess. I'm sorry."

"I'll miss you. Give my love to Uncle Peach."

"I don't think I will," Wheeler said.

When he had hung up, he sat still for a minute to think, and then he counted the few doomed bills that he had in his wallet.

Wheeler's earliest associations with Uncle Peach were among his privileges. In those days, when he was sober, and Wheeler only knew him sober in those days, Uncle Peach was a good-looking, good-humored man who could be charmingly attentive to a small boy. He was the first man Wheeler wanted to be like when he grew up.

"What do you want to be when you grow up?" his father asked him. It was after supper, and Wheeler was sitting in his father's lap by the kitchen stove.

"I want to be like Uncle Peach."

His father laughed. "Well, I'll be damned! You do, do you?"

And his mother said quietly, "Marce."

And then one night—it must not have been long after that, Wheeler must not have been more than five—he was waked up by a commotion in the house, and when he went to see what it was, he met his mother coming out of the spare bedroom, carrying a lamp.

"Go back to bed. Uncle Peach is sick."

"What's he got?"

"He's having one of his spells. Go back to bed, now, like I told you."

But he did not go back to bed. He went into the spare room where his mother had left Uncle Peach.

Uncle Peach had all his clothes off down to his underwear. "Hello, Wheeler boy," he said. "Uncle Peach is sick. Uncle Peach been going at a fast pace through the thorns and thistles that the ground has brought forth." And then he said, "*Oh*, me!"

Uncle Peach was standing in the middle of the floor, aiming at the bed, his feet wandering here and there and the rest of him staying mainly still.

"It's coming around!" he said. And he watched the bed and said again, "It's coming around!"

He made a mighty leap then toward the bed, but it was coming around too fast and he missed. He landed in the corner by the washstand, and lay there the way he fell, with his arms and legs strewn around him. Wheeler's mother came running back into the room. "Oh, Peach!" she said, in a way Wheeler had never heard her talk before. "What is *ever* to become of you?"

And Uncle Peach said, "Sing 'Yellow Rose o' Texas' to me, madam."

Uncle Peach was Dorie Catlett's trial. He was her baby brother. Their mother died when Peach was born, when Dorie, the oldest child, was thirteen. Their father never remarried. The story was that Andrew Wheeler had to take Peach to the field with him to plow when Peach was still a baby in arms. Andrew would take off his coat at the field edge, and spread it on the ground with his purse and all his money in one of its pockets and Peach asleep on top of it. Andrew's brother, James, would say later that if a thief had stolen Peach and all the money and left the coat, Andrew would have had the best of the trade. That was a story that Wheeler had often heard his mother tell. And she always quoted Uncle James and laughed, and then said, "Hmh!" not in refusal, Wheeler thought, but simply in dismissal; it was a judgment that she understood but did not find possible. She had had much of the raising of Peach, and he was her failure, or so she felt.

He never married, for the reason, according to him, that he could never accomplish a short courtship; no woman who came to know him well enough to make up her mind about him would make it up in his favor. And so his dependence on Dorie continued. He was always departing from her in a spirit of high resolve, going off, a new man, to seek his fortune, and always returning to her failed, drunk, sick, and broke, to be nursed to sobriety and health again, and reinfused with the notion that he was master of a better fate than available evidence encouraged even her to expect. He was her trial because she let him be, because she loved him and would not give him up.

He was Marce's trial for the opposite reason. Marce did not love him. He was constrained to be kind to him without benefit of love. He tolerated him, was patient with him, even helped him so far as he was able, for Dorie's sake, and for the sake of principle, but he found no excuse for him, and he gave up on him on fairly short acquaintance.

As a child, Wheeler was soon aware of his father's judgment and his mother's grief, and after the time when he wanted to be like Uncle Peach there was a time when he held him in gleeful contempt. Once, when Uncle Peach had come in drunk, and eaten, and fallen asleep in his chair, his head tilted back and his mouth open, Wheeler and his brother took the pepper shaker and half filled Uncle Peach's mouth with pepper, and Uncle Peach woke up after a while and said, "I feel like I'm going to sneeze!"

That was the last time Uncle Peach came to the house drunk. There must have been words between him and Marce about it, because after that Uncle Peach came sober and he came sick, but he did not come drunk.

When he worked, which was far from all the time, Uncle Peach was a carpenter, and for a while he was known as a good one. His failing in his younger years was merely infidelity. He was absolutely dependable as long as his pockets were empty. Money made him thirsty; once he got thirsty, he left; and then there was no getting him back until he had passed through flight, gallantry, drunkenness, devastation, and convalescence.

He was never a fast worker, but in his ponderous way, by much deliberation and some trial and error, he was capable of working well. People who were not in a hurry liked to hire him, for he cheapened his work in accordance with his own estimate of his faults, he was easy to get along with—was good company, in fact—and in the long run, if they had time for the long run, he satisfied his employers.

Later, as hopelessness and carelessness and perplexity grew upon him, his work became rougher. He declined gradually in public esteem until nobody would hire him to build a house, and declined further until nobody would hire him to build a barn. He became finally an odd-jobs man, a mender of leaky roofs, an overhauler of small outbuildings. He lost such habits of neatness and order as he had ever had, and worked in the midst of steadily increasing confusion. Whatever he was done with, for the day or the moment, he dropped wherever he was, until he built under his feet a sort of midden of lumber, scraps, and tools, in which whatever he needed at any given moment was lost.

In his puzzlement, he fell into the habit of talking to himself. He would go lurching and stumbling, sweating and puffing among the shambles of his work, picking up scraps and tools in one place, flinging them out of the way only to increase the disorder someplace else, muttering all the while to himself in steady commentary on his problem: "Now *where* did I put that damned saw? Did I lay it under here? No, sir. Did I lay it over *there*? *No*, sir. Well! I *had* it right *here* not a *minute* ago." Sometimes what he was looking for was in plain sight. Sometimes it was in his hand.

Once, when he was about fifteen, Wheeler watched Uncle Peach try to untangle a hundred feet of inch rope. Instead of imposing order on the tangle, he became more and more involved in it, until finally, trying to take up a length that was looped around his foot, he fell into the midst of it. What most impressed Wheeler at the time was that Uncle Peach was not embarrassed. He seemed too implicated in his clumsiness even to be aware of it. It was Wheeler who was embarrassed. Uncle Peach lay on his back, toiling like Laocoön among the interloopings of the rope, and Wheeler was astonished. It took him a year to see that it was funny.

And still, when Uncle Peach was down and sick and needed help, Dorie would help him. She would put him in bed in the spare room at home. Or he would send for her, and Marce would drive her in the buggy the ten miles to Uncle Peach's little farm over by Floyd's Station. The farm had been partly Marce's idea. He had encouraged and then helped Uncle Peach to buy it. It was the sort of place, Marce thought, that could put a sound footing under a tradesman's economy. And he probably thought too, or so Wheeler guessed, that the ten miles would put Uncle Peach out of the way. But if that was what he thought, he was mistaken; the distance was too short for impossibility and too long for convenience.

Seeing how his mother troubled herself with Uncle Peach and mourned over him, Wheeler said, bullying her in her own defense as a seventeen-year-old boy is apt to do, "To hell with him! Why don't you let him get on by himself the best way he can? What's he done for you?"

Dorie answered his first question, ignoring the second: "Because blood is thicker than water."

And Wheeler said, mocking her, "Blood is thicker than liquor."

"Yes," she said. "Thicker than liquor too."

The day was warm and clear, the sky an immaculate brilliance. The brighter leaves had all fallen, leaving only the oaks still darkly red or brown. After the long summer of drouth, there had been rain through the fall, and now the pastures were green. Wheeler had planned to end the day outdoors with his dog and gun. It was a day for which there were many better uses than the present one, and Wheeler was full of the bitterness of waste and loss. "Why don't I just leave the old son of a bitch down there?" he asked himself, driving too fast down the gravel road, a long white cloud of dust blooming behind him. And though he knew very well why, the question seemed to remain unanswered.

He wanted to be done with ordeals. The summer had been an ordeal. One hot, rainless day had followed another while pastures withered, crops parched, and ponds and springs went dry. Marce Catlett kept his stock alive by hauling water in barrels from the one spring that stayed constant. He hauled load after load, day after day, dipping the water out of the walled basin of the spring with a bucket. When he could leave the office early enough, Wheeler would drive up to help him, to ease the work a little and to keep him company.

One afternoon, when they had hauled the last load and poured the water into the trough for the cattle and were watching them drink, Marce looked at his son and smiled. "Awful, ain't it?"

"Yes," Wheeler said, and he did think so. Another merciless day was ending, the sun glared on the burnt world, the cattle were poor, the grass all but gone, and the sight depressed him.

"Well, I've seen dry years before this, and I'll tell you something. It's so miserable you think you'll never get over it. You're ready for the world to end. But it'll be past. There'll come a time when you won't think about it."

Marce raised his hat, ran his hand over his white hair, and put his hat back on, looking sideways, still smiling, at Wheeler.

They were sitting side by side on the edge of the wagon bed. The emptied barrels gleamed where water had spilled down their sides. All around them the late sunlight slanted brazenly over the greenless, dusty fields, and over the fly-covered backs of the lean steers. And Marce Catlett sat looking at his son with a light in his eye that came from another direction entirely, waiting to see if he saw.

It was a moment that would live with Wheeler for the rest of his life, for he saw his father then as he had at last grown old enough to see him, not only as he declared himself, but as he was. And in that seeing Wheeler became aware of a pattern, that his father both embodied and was embodied in, that also contained the drouth and made light of it, that contained other hardships also and made light of them. For his father's good work was on that place in a way that granted and collaborated in its own endurance, that had carried them thus far, and would carry them on. Looking at his father, Wheeler knew, and would not forget, that though they were surrounded by the marks and leavings of a bad year, they were surrounded also by the marks and leavings of good work, which for that year and any other proposed an end and a new beginning.

He slowed down as he entered the town of Langlay. In the center of town he turned off the main road, drove to the railroad station, and parked his car. He did not have long to wait to catch the interurban, and soon he was seated in a nearly empty car, looking out the windows at the farms and little towns as the railjoints clicked under the wheels.

It seemed to him that for the last hour he had been passing through the stages of an abandonment of his own will, working his way toward a leap past which his own wishes would be mere idle dreams. At each stage, it seemed to him, turning back had become less possible. Now, sliding down toward the city along the same tracks that Uncle Peach had followed days ago, it was easy for Wheeler to imagine himself telling the desk clerk, "I don't know anybody named Leonidas Wheeler." But he knew better than that. He knew that he had not passed the place of turning back that day, or that year. He may, he thought, have been born on the downhill side of it.

When Wheeler headed home from law school, he did not have Uncle Peach much in mind, one way or another. But when he arrived, there was Uncle Peach, older, grayer, and worse for wear, traveling at a slower pace now among the thorns and thistles that the ground brought forth, but still on the same route. And Dorie was still seeing him through.

"Blood is thicker than liquor," Wheeler said to her, no longer mocking, but gently stating the fact as he knew she saw it.

"Yes," she said, and smiled. "It is."

And as he knew by then, she had more than that in mind. Uncle Peach was, she thought, "one of the least of these my brethren"—a qualification for her care that the blood connection only compounded. If one of the least of Christ's brethren happened to be her brother, then the obligation was as clear as the penalty. She had long ago given up hope for Uncle Peach. She cared for him without hope, because she had passed the place of turning back or looking back. Quietly, almost submissively, she propped herself against him, because in her fate and faith she was opposed to his ruin.

Marce, who was the most craftsmanly of farmers, the artist of his particular domain of earth and flesh, stood outside this push and pull of opposition. He was Uncle Peach's opposite, all right, but the pith of Marce's character was perhaps his ability to stand opposite without opposing. Dorie opposed Uncle Peach because she loved him. Wheeler had opposed him, so far, because he was affronted by him. Marce merely maintained his difference. He was a man of simple preferences and complex abilities—a better carpenter, for instance, in answer to his own occasional need to be one, than Uncle Peach had ever been. He simply knew what he desired, and worked toward it with whatever means he had, without fuss. Not having inherited Uncle Peach, he patiently tolerated as much of him as he thought tolerable. The rest he ignored.

Wheeler, who loved his father and liked his ways, assumed that he thought and felt as his father did. But when he returned home, Uncle Peach devolved upon him. He was perhaps made eligible to come into this inheritance by the ownership of an automobile, which, as it turned out, proved the finest windfall of Uncle Peach's entire drinking career. It meant that he could get drunk in complete peace of mind. He could go clear to Louisville, spend all his money,

exhaust his credit, ruin his health—and then Wheeler would come
and take him home in the car, paying off whatever creditors might
stand in the way. It was a grand improvement over the horse-and-
buggy days.

When the train stopped, Wheeler stepped off so quickly that he did
not stop. He went through the station to the street, and set off on
foot for the hotel, too impatient to wait for a streetcar. He went
through the Haymarket, stepping past boxes and bags and bins and
baskets of produce, crates of eggs, chickens in cages along the edge
of the sidewalk. And then, the street opening in front of him again,
free of encumbrances, he went on toward the stockyards and its sat-
ellite businesses and shops catering to the needs and the weaknesses
of country people.

He came to the hotel, a turreted corner building of dingy ele-
gance, with its name in white block letters on windows and door,
went in, and stopped and let the door shut behind him. He stopped
because at that point he had come to a place he would never have
come to on his own. He had been there before, for the same reason,
and the lobby was familiar to him: the white tiled floor mopped
with dirty water, the black wainscoting, the hard chairs pushed
back to the walls, the spittoons gaping up at the pressed-metal
ceiling—a room meager and stark from the expectation of hard
use. In the chairs a few men merely sat, as they had been sitting, so
far as Wheeler could tell, when he was there last, and might sit
forever.

Behind the desk, the clerk stood leaning against a wall of pigeon-
holes, reading a newspaper. When Wheeler crossed the lobby and
stopped at the desk, it seemed to him that he came to the end of the
slant he had been on; now he spoke the words that sent him, like a
diver, into the air: "Mr. Leonidas Wheeler?"

"Oh," the clerk said, looking up and folding his paper, "you must be Mr. Catlett." He fingered his ledger.

"What's his bill?"

The clerk named the sum, and Wheeler paid.

"Thank you very much, sir."

And then the clerk spoke to a Negro porter who was mopping the floor in the hallway off the lobby: "Take him up. Mr. Wheeler's room."

"This way, sir," the porter said, and led the way to the elevator in long, pushing strides. He held the door for Wheeler, and then shut it, and they started up.

"You Mr. Wheeler's kinfolks?" the porter asked over the bumping and groaning of the elevator.

"I'm his nephew."

The porter gave a somewhat embarrassed laugh, as unwilling to intrude as to leave Wheeler unwarned. "Mr. Wheeler done got hisself plumb down."

Before the elevator even reached the floor where Uncle Peach's room was, Wheeler could hear him roaring. "Oh ho ho ho!" he was saying. "Oh, Lord! Oh, me! Oh ho ho ho ho!"

Wheeler glanced at the porter, who smiled obligingly and said, "He been doing that quite some time."

When they unlocked the door and went in, Uncle Peach never even heard them. It was a tiny room, its one window looking out at a blank wall across an alley, and it was as much a shambles as one man could have made it without the use of tools. The room's one table and chair were turned over on the floor. Uncle Peach's pants, shirt, shoes, socks, necktie, coat, and hat were scattered all over it. Bedclothes and pillows had been flung off the bed in several directions. Beside the sagging bed was a wastebasket that Uncle Peach had attempted to vomit into, but missed. Uncle Peach was lying on the bed under a blanket with his feet sticking out, his face a mess, his eyes shut tight, still hollering.

"Be still, Uncle Peach!" Wheeler said sharply.

Uncle Peach instantly quieted down.

"Huh?" he said. "Who is it?"

"It's Wheeler. What in the world have you done to yourself?"

"You know damned good and well what I've done to myself."

"I got your message," Wheeler said. "Are you ready to go home?"

Uncle Peach groaned. He lay still a moment. And then he opened his eyes and looked at Wheeler. He cleared his throat. "I'm ready, Wheeler boy, but I've got to have a drink before I can move." As his way was at such times, he spoke of himself so matter-of-factly that Wheeler knew he was telling the truth.

Wheeler turned to the porter, who was still standing in the open door. "Can you give him a bath and a shave?"

"Yes, sir. For a consideration."

Wheeler grinned at the delicacy of that. "What do you consider a consideration?"

"One dollar."

Wheeler handed him a dollar. "As cold as possible," he said.

In the street again, Wheeler stopped to think. He knew beyond doubt, having seen the evidence, that whiskey was within reach, but he did not know where to find it. He had not asked Uncle Peach for directions because he knew that Uncle Peach's directions, even when he was sober, were not followable. He was almost ready to turn back and lay his problem before the desk clerk, when he saw a man coming toward him in a swaying, hobbling gait that he recognized unmistakably. It was Laban Jones, Wheeler's friend from childhood, a Port William farmer's son, crippled from birth, who was working in an office at the stockyards. Wheeler caught his arm. "Laban," he said. The face that turned to look at him was as sweet and honest as the day itself.

"Why, hello, Wheeler. How in the world are you?"

"All right," Wheeler said. "*Nearly* all right. I need a half-pint of whiskey, and I don't know where to find it."

"*You* do, Wheeler?" Laban laughed. As always his hat was set far back on his head as if that was just the place he kept it in case he might want to put it on.

Wheeler laughed too. "I *may* need it before this is over. But at present Uncle Peach is the one in need."

Laban widened his eyes and nodded. "I see. You've got to patch him up and get him home."

"That's right."

"Well, come with me."

Laban turned and started back the way he had come, hobbling along at a pace Wheeler had to hurry to keep up with. Laban's eagerness to be of use was familiar to Wheeler, but it was strange to him to have Laban as a guide. Always before, it had been the other way around. Wheeler had been the one who knew, Laban the innocent who learned late. Once he had actually sawed off a tree limb that a squirrel was on, forgetting that he himself was standing on the same limb. Now he was guiding Wheeler through the invisible world that lay beneath the visible one. Wheeler walked along beside him obediently and asked no questions.

They went several blocks, and then Laban abruptly entered a hardware store. Wheeler walking behind him now, they went through the store, through a large stockroom at the back, winding their way among stacks of boxes, crates, and kegs. And then Laban opened another door and they emerged in the bottom of what appeared to be a deep shaft, brick walled, with a tiny patch of sky at the top. It was a dark, damp place, smelling of mold, as hidden from the rest of the world as the bottom of a well. The place astonished Wheeler, and he was grateful not to be alone.

Laban pointed to a ragged hole in one of the brick walls. "Hand a dollar bill through that hole."

"Through that hole," Wheeler said.

Laban was grinning, greatly amused. "That's right."

Wheeler did as he was told, although, as much as he trusted Laban, he did not do so gladly. But he felt the bill gently withdrawn from his fingers, and felt the cold glass of a small bottle pressed firmly upon the palm of his hand.

He slipped the bottle into his pocket, and followed Laban back out along the meander they had come in by and into the daylit street.

"Well, that ought to fix him up," Laban said. "He'll be a new man now."

"He's been a new man many a time before this," Wheeler said. "Thanks."

"My pleasure," Laban said, and hobbled away before Wheeler could ask the question he had in mind.

Uncle Peach, scrubbed, shaved, and reassembled in his blue suit and tie, his hat, reshaped, on his knee, was sitting in the chair in the middle of the room, which the porter was now setting to rights. The suit was the only one Uncle Peach had; he used it only to get drunk in. It was a garment a man could feel comfortable either wearing or walking on, as need might be. And Uncle Peach looked as old and exhausted as his suit, pale and wasted, his neck too small for his collar. And yet his head, despite its snow-white hair, was somehow still a boy's head, the ears sticking innocently too far out, the hair, which had been wetted and combed down, already drying and rising stiffly like the hackles on a dog's neck. Wheeler could see a crooked vein pulsing at his temple.

"Here," he said. "See if that'll help."

Uncle Peach held the bottle of colorless whiskey up, trembling, against the window light, and looked through it, and then he pulled the cork and drank. "Ah!" he said, and made a face.

Wheeler took the bottle back.

"*Ter*'ble stuff! *Aw*ful stuff!" Uncle Peach said, fighting for breath.

"But you like it," Wheeler said and laughed. He had begun to feel a little relieved; he was involved in the problem now, getting something done.

"I like a little from time to time," Uncle Peach said, and then, feeling a sudden access of moral seriousness, he said to Wheeler and the porter and anyone who might be passing by in the hall, "But don't never drink, my boys. Stay clean away from it."

And then the three of them stayed quiet for what must have been several minutes in that little room that, even straightened up, oppressed Wheeler by its measliness, Wheeler and the porter watching Uncle Peach who was staring at the window. Slowly he seemed to grow steadier within himself. He took a deep, tremulous breath and smacked his mouth as though tasting the air. And then he reached for the bottle. "Bird can't fly with one wing, Wheeler boy."

Wheeler, who had flight in mind, let him have another drink. But when he took the bottle back that time he handed it to the porter. "That's all," he said to Uncle Peach.

"That's all," Uncle Peach said, in a tone of finality in which Wheeler recognized the familiar intention of reform. For a while now Uncle Peach would be a prohibitionist, a new man. "I'm going to wipe the slate clean! Damn, I am! Work ever' day! Eat and sleep reg'lar!"

But far from flying, when they put his hat on and helped him up, Uncle Peach collapsed back onto the chair and would have continued to the floor, had they not held him. He shook his head. "Whoo!"

"You're going to have to work at this," Wheeler told him. "Pay attention."

Uncle Peach paid attention, and when they got him up again, he stood. They walked him out to the elevator, they descended with him to the lobby, and then the porter walked ahead and held open the street door.

If he could keep Uncle Peach on his feet, Wheeler was determined to walk to the station. Uncle Peach needed the effort and the fresh air, Wheeler thought, and he was right, for as they went along Uncle Peach recovered some of his capabilities. He was not standing up on his own, but he was walking on his own. And Wheeler began to be a little hopeful. Maybe, he thought, he could get Uncle Peach back in charge of himself by nightfall. Wheeler wanted to go home. He imagined himself finally free of this story he was in, telling it to Bess. Encumbered as he was, he imagined how neatly and nimbly *she* would walk beside him.

As he and Uncle Peach made their way slowly along, they necessarily attracted the attention of the passersby—a handsome, erect, nicely dressed young man walking arm in arm with an aging drunk. Wheeler bore it well enough, for he had expected to have to, and he knew there was no escape. But the pressure of so many curious, amused, or disapproving stares produced in Uncle Peach a desire to rise above his condition. If he was a man who obviously *did* disgrace and degrade himself with drink, he wished at least to appear to be a man who *knew* that he should not.

"My boy," he said loudly, "there's a moral lesson in this for you, if you'll only learn it. Here's a awful example right before your eyes."

"Hush," Wheeler said. "Just please hush."

But Uncle Peach's heart was full. His voice was trembling. "You got a good mother and daddy. Finest a man ever had. You don't have to be like old Uncle Peach. Let this be a lesson to you, Wheeler boy. I know what a life like mine goes to show."

"For God's *sake*, be quiet," Wheeler said. And then, though he knew better, he said, "Lesson to *me*! If it's no lesson to you, why should it be a lesson to me?"

"It *is* a lesson to me. I've learnt it a thousand times."

Wheeler usually put up with Uncle Peach by finding him funny, which was easy enough, for Uncle Peach's life and conversation were rich in absurdities, and Wheeler's involvements with him invariably made good stories. But underlying the possibility of laughter was the possibility of anger, and he was close to that now. He did not need a moral lesson from Uncle Peach. He did not need Uncle Peach, so far as he was aware, for anything—not him nor the likes of him. So far as he was aware, nobody did.

"There's no moral lesson in a man's inability to learn a moral lesson," he said, and wondered if that was true. But Uncle Peach's thoughts had strayed to other matters; if he heard, he did not answer.

The train was crowded, people were standing in the aisle, and the car was hot. Wheeler tried to open a window, but cold weather had come officially, if not in fact, and the windows had been locked shut.

When the train gained speed outside the city and the car began to sway, Uncle Peach became sick again. He swallowed and smacked his mouth, and drops of sweat ran down his face. Wheeler looked for a way out, perhaps to the vestibule at the end of the car, but with the aisle full of people escape appeared to be impossible, and anyhow it was too late, for suddenly Uncle Peach leaned forward and, with awful retches and groans, vomited between his spread knees. Wheeler caught hold of him and held him. All around them people were giving them looks and drawing their feet away. Wheeler gave Uncle Peach his handkerchief, helped him out of his coat, and fanned him with his hat, encouraging and helping him the best he could. But the spasms came repeatedly, with unabated violence, and with each one Uncle Peach's gasps and groans and roars of supplication became louder. "Ohhhh, Lord!" he said. "Ohhhh, me! Ohhhh, Lord, help me!" Wheeler's pleadings with him to be quiet might as well have been addressed to a panic-stricken horse. As soon as he would be almost recovered and quiet, suddenly he would lean forward again. "Uuuuuup! *Oh,* my God!" And when the spasm passed he would roll his head against the seatback. "Ohhhh, me!"

It was an awful intimacy carried on in public. To Wheeler, it was endurable only because it was inescapable. He knew that Uncle Peach was suffering, and yet his suffering seemed merely the cause, the relatively minor cause, of the calamitous uproar that he was filling the whole car with. And yet, in the very midst of it, Wheeler knew that it was rare. It would make a good story, as soon as he could get out of it. But it was not funny now.

Once they had landed, mercifully, on the station platform at Langlay, Wheeler steadied Uncle Peach a moment to let him secure his balance, and then he said, "Let's go."

"All right," Uncle Peach said.

His hand caught firmly under Uncle Peach's arm, Wheeler

turned then to walk to his car, only to feel Uncle Peach turn in the opposite direction, a difference of intention that came close to bringing them both down.

"*What are you doing?*" Wheeler said, angry sure enough now.

"Got to get the old mare and buggy."

Wheeler turned him loose, half hoping he would fall, for Uncle Peach, who had used up the afternoon, had now laid claim to the night as well. Wheeler was not going to get home by breakfast, let alone supper. His leap had not ended yet. "Well, damn it to hell!" he said. "Let's go get the damned old mare."

"*Got* to get her," Uncle Peach said. "Got to *have* her."

And so they went to the livery stable and had Uncle Peach's old sorrel mare, Godiva, harnessed and hitched to the buggy. Wheeler paid the bill there too, and they started for Uncle Peach's place, Wheeler driving and Uncle Peach leaning back in the seat, holding on.

It was a long six miles. Uncle Peach's stomach objected as strenuously to the motion of the buggy as it had to that of the train. He had long ago emptied himself, but the spasms came anyhow, prolonged clenches that left him fighting for balance and breath. And each time, Wheeler had to stop the mare and hold Uncle Peach to keep him from falling out of the buggy.

Finally, after this had happened perhaps half a dozen times, Wheeler, who had remained angry, said, "I hope you puke your damned guts out."

And Uncle Peach, who lay, quaking and white, against the seat-back, said, "Oh, Lord, honey, you can't mean that."

As if his anger had finally stripped all else away, suddenly Wheeler saw Uncle Peach as perhaps Dorie had always seen him—a poor, hurt, weak mortal, twice hurt because he *knew* himself to be hurt and weak and mortal. And then Wheeler knew what he did need from Uncle Peach. He needed him to be comforted. That was all. He put his arm around Uncle Peach, then, and patted him as if he were a child. "No," he said. "I don't mean it."

When they got to the house it was almost nightfall. Wheeler left the mare standing at the back door while he helped Uncle Peach into the house. It was a bachelor's house, rudimentary, spare, unadorned, and, on top of that, a mess, for as he always did, Uncle Peach had lost interest in housekeeping as he gained interest in travel. Wheeler led him to a chair, and then he straightened the bedclothes on the bed and took off Uncle Peach's shoes and helped him to lie down.

In the failing light he drove the mare to the barn, unhitched her, watered her at the cistern trough, unharnessed and fed her. She applied herself to her supper as though all were well.

Uncle Peach's little farm had always endeared itself to Wheeler, and he could remember when Uncle Peach had kept it moderately well. Now, like Uncle Peach himself, it was running down. The fences barely served to contain and the brushy pastures to feed the one old mare. The garden was ragged with tall frost-killed weeds. The tobacco crop was hanging cured in the barn, poorer than the year.

Lying on the bed in the lamplight, Uncle Peach looked like a corpse, and lay as still as one. Wheeler stood and watched him a moment to make sure he was breathing. And then he lighted a lamp in the kitchen and moved around for some time, straightening the place up. He drew a fresh bucket of water from the well, drank, and built a fire in the cooking stove. But when he searched the kitchen for food he found nothing except—under a cloth spread over the table—a jar of jam, half a can of pork and beans covered with gray mold like a mouse's pelt, and most of a box of stale crackers.

"Well, *damn* it!" he said, for he was hungry himself, and he knew he needed to get something in the way of food into Uncle Peach. He lighted the lantern that he found beside the woodbox, and went out. Searching the henhouse, the hayloft, and every trough and manger in the barn, he found five eggs.

As he walked back to the house, carrying the eggs in his hat, peering beyond the lantern light into the dark and the rising wind, it seemed to him strange beyond belief that he was where he was, doing what he was doing. It seemed to him that he was still in his leap, still falling, still attached to Uncle Peach, who was still falling. Sooner or later they would hit bottom together and could start climbing out. He did not know when. He did not know how he was going to get back to his car. All the world to him now was the darkness and the wind, himself and Uncle Peach—two needy men and five eggs. Between the stars and the ground the only lights he could see were his own and the lighted windows of Uncle Peach's house. The only sound was the long breath of the wind in the top of the old locust by the back door. He no longer thought of telling his story to Bess. He only missed her. He missed his life.

He was glad to get back inside, where the stove had made it warm. He scrambled the eggs, and warmed some of the crackers in the oven to make them crisp again. He got Uncle Peach up and fed him, and ate what was left himself. He found clean sheets and remade the bed, and helped Uncle Peach to undress and get under the covers. He quickly washed the dishes they had used, thinking to have a little time, finally, to sit down in and be still.

But Uncle Peach began to dream bad dreams, struggling and crying out in his sleep: "*Oh*! Lord God, I see him a-coming! On his old smoky horse!" And Wheeler lay down beside him to quiet him. For a while he did sleep quietly, and then his dreams returned again. Wheeler was awake for hours, soothing and consoling Uncle Peach when he fretted and muttered and cried out, striving with him when he fought.

And so they waged the night, Uncle Peach striving with the Devil, Wheeler striving with Uncle Peach. It seemed to Wheeler that the two of them were lost together there in the dark house in the dark sky. He could not have told the time within three hours.

Once, after they had struggled through yet another nightmare, Uncle Peach, who had momentarily waked, said slowly into the darkness, "Wheeler boy, this is a hell of a way for a young man just married to have to pass the night."

"I thought of that," Wheeler said. "But it's all right." And he patted Uncle Peach, who went back to sleep and for a while was quiet.

Later, Wheeler himself went to sleep, his hand remaining on Uncle Peach's shoulder where it had come to rest.

And that is where daylight found him, far from home.

Where Did They Go?

(1947)

For every day he lived, my father could imagine two or three others that he would like to live if he did not have to do what he had to do. "Your father," my mother used to say to my brother and me, to explain him to us, "has eyes bigger than his stomach." We understood that, and it did not seem strange to us that most of our mornings, on schoolyear weekends and in summer, would begin with a summons to the bathroom where our father would be shaving and thinking. "Andy!" he would say. "Henry! Come here, boys."

As we stood at his elbows, he would describe for us in detail a day, impossible for himself, that he nonetheless had in mind. Some would be workdays, and he would talk his way through a set of little jobs at the farm that he did not have time to do himself, anticipating problems, solutions, and incidental satisfactions. Others were pleasure days, and he would tell us how he thought a certain pond or the holes in a certain creek might be successfully fished, or where there was a hickory tree loaded with nuts, or where we might find a covey of birds. As he hurriedly applied the lather to his face, shaved, and dressed for his day at the office, he would loiter over the details: from what direction to approach the covey, how to manage the dog; what kind of pole and what kind of bait to use, by the roots of which old tree we should drop in our lines. The workday instructions were orders. The others were suggestions; he was telling us what he would do if he were us and had the happiness of living that day outside the demands of his particular life. We were to be his delegates to the great realm of possibility.

Of course, the world and the imagination being what they are, we often failed him—mismanaged his instructions, or refused to take his suggestions. But his was a practical imagination, and sometimes we succeeded. Even when we failed them, his imaginings remained with us, so that we inherited from him early his abounding sense of the possibilities of the countryside lying around our town of Port William. After forty years I can recollect, as vividly as if they had happened, a number of hunting and fishing jaunts that he imagined and none of us ever made.

After he bought the old Mack Crayton place in 1947, and established Jake and Minnie Branch and their swarming household upon it, it was news but no surprise to me when he called me into the bathroom one May morning to tell me that I was to work for Jake Branch that summer as a hired hand. The old Crayton place was badly run down; my father had bought it partly because of his vision of how it would look cleaned up and put to rights. It was a job of work that he would have loved to take part in, would not have time to take part in, and was therefore sending me to take part in, with his proxy, so to speak, not as the bearer of his authority, but as the heir of his imagined joy.

That this was to be a part of my education, I also understood. My father's strongest-held theory of education was that if Henry and I could learn the use of our hands, then, whatever might happen to us as a result of the use or misuse of our heads, we at least need not starve. From Jake Branch—and from Elton Penn, the Coulters, my grandfathers, my father himself—I did learn the use of my hands. But when he put me under the tutelage of Jake Branch, my father in effect abandoned me to a vast and chancy curriculum of which nobody was in charge.

This plan of my father's suited me as well as it did him, probably better, though for a different reason. My reason was that it would put me for the whole summer in the company of R. T., Minnie Branch's youngest son by her first marriage. From the neck down, R. T. looked as I, at the age of thirteen, would have died to look. He looked, from the neck down, like Michelangelo's *David*. From the neck up, he looked like nothing on earth but himself. He had a nose that appeared to have been pushed hard onto his face by God's thumb. He had a head full of brown hair as stiff and directionless as a pile of jackstraws. His tongue lived in the corner of his mouth, hospitable to the occasional gnat or fly that lit there to drink. He was sixteen and had been, in body, a grown man for three or four years. I admired him unequivocally. When he discovered my awe of him, there was virtually no limit to the stunts he undertook to amuse me: catch and ride bridleless an unbroke two-year-old mule, or run headfirst under a sizable rick of baled hay, or lift off the ground the hind legs of a Jersey cow that Jake Branch happened at the time to be milking. The latter feat earned him a lick over the head with the milking stool that would have felled an ordinary ox, but not R. T., who merely staggered loose from the cow, and, crossing his eyes, donated his pain and suffering to the good cause of my amusement.

Besides R. T. and Minnie and Jake, there was also R. T.'s fifteen-year-old sister, Ester, the youngest of Minnie's first family of six, only the two of whom were still living at home. Ester was a big girl for her age, who seemed forever at work in the kitchen, where, heaven knows, there was an endless amount of work to do. She favored me, every time I looked at her, with a wild giggle, which made me feel that I was party to a conspiracy that I had not heard about, which made me blush, which made her giggle, until Minnie would tell her, "Shut up, girl! Leave him alone!"

And there were Lillybelle and Col Oaks, Lillybelle one of the eight children of Jake's first set, and Col her husband, whose style she no longer even tried to live up to. Col was a dandy. His attention to himself—to what a more vulgar time would call his "image"—would have been almost ladylike, had it not been so clearly the result of a monopolizing male vanity. There was a precision of self-adulation in the way he rolled a smoke, the way he rolled his sleeves, the way he cocked his hat, the way he grinned around a matchstick held delicately always between the same pair of incisors, the way his voice quavered when he sang "Born to Lose" or "When Your Blue Moon Once Again Has Turned to Gold." A hundred times a day, Col would lift his hat in a three-fingered pinch as exquisite as a jeweler's, toss back his languorous forelock, and replace the hat as though preparing to meet, if not his Maker, perhaps the press. This procedure required him to stop absolutely whatever he might be doing, and was almost routinely concluded by a curse from his father-in-law, who in the meantime might have been holding up one end of a log. The smooth underside of Col's right forearm bore the tattoo of a scantily clad lady who danced when Col flexed his muscles, and in the midst of work he would sometimes spend long minutes studying it, slowly doubling and relaxing his fist, whether entranced by the loveliness of his own arm or by the lady who danced there, I could not tell. For these and other reasons, Jake had renamed him Noah. Noah Count.

With the same justice, he called Lillybelle Mrs. Noah Count. Lillybelle spent most of her time at odds with her father over his re-marriage, and consequently at odds with Minnie, and with all the rest of the house. She stayed all day, when they would let her, in her and Col's upstairs room where they did "light housekeeping." She was childless, bitterly jolly, disappointed, lazy, and mean—mad at everybody, jealous of Col, afraid of the dark. I used to visit her sometimes because she was always nice to me and I liked to hear the things she would say about the others. She would be sitting, fat and sad, in her yellow chenille bathrobe, her hair in curlers, eating pear preserves out of the jar with a long spoon, without benefit of bread, "just making it through to Saturday night." On Saturday night, when she and Col would go down to Hargrave to the double fea-ture and other social attractions, she would emerge from their room done up in lipstick and curls and high heels, smelling, Jake said, "like two rose bushes and one honeysuckle."

There were also Jake's and Minnie's own children: Angeleen, Beureen, Coreen, Delano (who had by fate of gender escaped being Doreen), the twins, Eveleen and Franklin (alias Floreen), and one soon to be born, already named Gloreen or Grover, as the case might be—"all of 'em the same age," my father said, "or damn near it." To say that Minnie was fertile would be an understatement. Her womb was the horn of plenty itself, from which her babes leapt, as my father maintained, after only five months, wide-eyed and yell-ing vigorously, ready, according to Jake, to go to work, milking and spreading manure. Jake was awed by his prowess as a sire. "They going to have to *do* something about me," he would say gaily. "All I got to do is *look* at her."

That was the regular family membership. But in that spring of 1947 there was also Reenie, Jake's youngest child by his first wife, who still lived with her mother at Hargrave, and who had come to visit and to help set out the crop. Reenie was eighteen that spring, a small, beautifully made, brash talking girl with freckles across her nose and short brown curls that filled with red lights when the sun shone on them. R. T., I knew, was in love with her. "Reenie" was short for Irene, and it was Reenie's prettiness, I think, that had suggested to Minnie the ideal of a string of girl children, alphabetically ordered, all named something-een.

There was, finally, Leaf Trim, Jake's full-time hired hand—hired, Jake said, because he had to have *somebody* who both knew how to work and would. Leaf lived in the room above the kitchen, reached by a narrow, steep stair between the back porch and the kitchen wall. I went up there once with R. T., and I remember how that room astonished me. Its sole piece of furniture was a large wooden bedstead covered with a strawtick ripped down the side and leaking straw onto the floor. It was a room as unceremoniously occupied as a stall in the barn.

Leaf was a gaping stutterer and a veteran of World War I. He had been to Paris, and he told R. T. and me stories of French ladies who did a dance of couples called the jigjig—only Leaf, because of his speech impediment, sang the word and made it rather lyrical: "Ji-igji-ig." That jigjigging in Paris, it seemed, had been the high point of his life, for the ladies there, he said, "di-id it be-etter than mm-ah-anything you e-ever sa-aw." The subject fascinated R. T., and embarrassed him, made him put his cap on crossways and grin and bite his tongue. I ingratiated myself with him by cross-examining Leaf closely on the subject of jigjigging. "Ask him what she done after that," R. T. would whisper, and I would ask, and Leaf would tell.

This had been a subject keenly interesting to me and my schoolmates for some time. We were aware of girls off yonder in their world, and we supposed that eventually there was going to be some sort of meeting between our kind and their kind. We had heard a good deal about jigjigging, under different names, and we talked about it a good deal. We knew that it happened among the animals. We assumed that it had happened among our parents, and that we were the results, but we had very little in the way of empirical evidence. One of the boys in our class had seen his parents performing the jigjig, or something like it, in a dry creek bed, but it is hard to establish common usage on the basis of a single instance. I had hoped that R. T. might be able to help, but if R. T. was better informed than I was, he would not admit it, and he was not of a speculative turn of mind. And so I was delighted to receive Leaf Trim's testimony, even if it did imply that jigjigging was an activity that went on mostly in foreign countries. I wondered if Leaf's own jigjigging days were not about over, in any case, for he had lost several front teeth and tobacco juice was usually glistening in the creases of his chin.

Though talking put Leaf to extreme effort, tightening the cords of his neck, when he sang his voice came sweet and free. To hear him stop talking, which he seldom did, and start to sing "The Wabash Cannonball" or "Amazing Grace" always seemed a sort of miracle to me, as if a groundhog had suddenly soared into the air like a swallow. "Leaf" was a merciful foreshortening of Lafayette, which would have been a fancy mouthful for poor Leaf, if he had ever said it.

There was a big weatherboarded frame house on the Crayton place then, burned down now, and Jake Branch's domestic enterprise had filled it to overflowing. There was not an empty or a still or a quiet corner in it. It was always full of clatters, shouts, scrapes, laughs, cries, screams, songs, grunts, snores, blows, jars, and shocks of every kind. This wondrous commotion was, in a manner of speaking, overseen by a great spreading white oak, a member of the old original forest, that stood in the yard and shaded the porch and the front of the house in the afternoon. Burned when the house burned, it was a glorious tree. On fair days in warm weather much of the work and most of the social life of the household went on under it. I had not grown far enough from childhood to make much of coincidences; to me, it seemed merely appropriate that people named Oaks and Branch and Leaf should live under an oak tree.

When my father let me out of the car early in the morning, and I walked back the driveway past the house to the barn, I could usually hear Minnie talking in the house. She had a carrying voice that always rode the edge of hilarity or calamity—in its ordinary conversational range, if the weather was quiet, you could stand half a mile away and understand every word she said—and most of her household talk consisted of commands: "Delano, *get* that damned old nasty mop out of that baby's *face*! Angeleen, is *that* what you call *sweeping*? Ester, *hurry* up now and get them dishes done! Beureen! *Get* out of them ashes! I *told* you!" And then she might start whistling, as sweetly as if she were off somewhere in the woods by herself. She could whistle anything, trilling it out like a bird; you wanted to stop and listen. "Don't never go nowhere in the dark with a whistling woman," Jake liked to say to me in her presence, and wink and shake his head.

I would go on back to the barn where they would have the mules harnessed and ready to go to the field, usually, by the time I got there, and Jake would tell me what he wanted me to do. He made it a point of honor not to treat me as the boss's son. "Wheeler," he said to my father, "I'll treat him just like he was my own boy," a proposition to which I thought my father agreed too readily. Though Jake did not swing at me with whatever he happened to have in his hand, which was his way, frequently, of bringing R. T. back to reality, at times he did, as he put it, speak to me "pretty plain." "*Now* what in the hell are you doing, Andy?" he would say, or, "What you need for that is your little ass kicked." And once when I had taken off my shirt in imitation of R. T., Jake looked down at my physique from his seat on the tobacco-setter barrel, spat over the wheel, and pronounced: "*Mouse* tits!"

He could be kind too, and sometimes was, even to Col, and he was the first man who ever trusted me to work by myself. Later that same summer he sent me to the tobacco patch with a hoe and a file and a jug of water. "When you can step on the head of your shadow, Andy, come to the house for dinner." I found that I could not lengthen my leg, and that only the implacable climb of the sun toward meridian could shorten my shadow. And so I learned that I lived under law, as if my father had not already told me.

When I got out of school and began work for Jake that year, they were setting out the tobacco crop. It was a big crop, and Jake was in a sort of ecstasy compounded of pleasure over what he had done, worry over what he still had to do, and outrage at what fate had given him in the way of help. We were as oddly assorted a crew as ever went to the field: Col full of persnickety self-regard; Lillybelle sulking, a scarf tied over her curlers; Leaf with his stutter; Reenie dressed, every day, as if it were Saturday night; R. T. with his cap on sideways, tongue in the corner of his mouth, eyes on Reenie; and I, who that summer weighed about ninety pounds, and was, as Jake plainly told me several times a day, "too short in the push-up."

It would have to be said for us, at least, that we worked. It would have to be said for Jake that he got it out of us somehow. We used the setter when the weather was good, and when it rained we set the plants in the muddy rows by hand. When it rained we went to the field barefooted, and stayed wet. Nothing except the occasional downpour stopped us, and then, having no shelter, we stood in the rain until it slacked up, and went back to work. We did not miss a day.

We worked, and we ate. There was never anything like the meals we sat down to at the big table in Minnie Branch's kitchen. The mornings would have begun there with a great commerce between kitchen and garden and smokehouse and chicken house and cellar. Even the young children would be put to picking and plucking and fixing. The result would be a quantity of food that you would be surprised at when you saw it laid out on the table, and surprised again to see how quickly it was eaten up. Minnie would put the biscuits on the table heaped up in a washpan, and they would vanish beneath a cascade of forks. The thought of reaching for one barehanded was almost more than you could stand. There would be thirteen or fourteen of us at the table, Ester standing at the stove to wait on us, Jake at the head of the table, Minnie at the foot with the baby on her lap, the rest of us sitting anywhere we could on everything from high chairs to beehives. The house's indigenous uproar of voices and noises did not stop. It did not stop for anything. We ate, straggled out to the barn, watered the mules, hitched them up again, and went back to work.

Jake's triumph that year was that he had Col and Lillybelle working on the setter. He had accomplished this by great practical and psychological cunning, which he acknowledged to me by many stealthy winks and grins, but he could not help saying to me, once, to their faces: "Damn, Andy, I got 'em where I want 'em now!" He had them where he wanted them because he had them in his power;

because he drove the setter, he could see to it that they did not stop work for any frivolous reason, and he drove at a pace that nudged relentlessly at the limits of their speed and endurance. The big black mules drew the setter down one long row after another, and Col and Lillybelle rode the low seats with their laps full of plants, placing them one at a time into the ground, grumbling and muttering at Jake's heedless back.

Each morning, when we had got enough plants pulled from the bed to get the setter started, Jake and Col and Lillybelle would start setting, Leaf would take three mules and the disk and prepare the ground ahead of the setter, R. T. would take another team and keep the setter supplied with water and plants. And Reenie and I would continue pulling plants from the beds, helped out by Leaf and R. T. when they had time to spare.

It was pretty work when you had time to think about it, and weren't too tired to care. We drew the white-stemmed, green-leafed plants out of the moist ground of the beds, and laid them neatly in bushel baskets and old washtubs. R. T. hauled them to the patch where the setter crew spaced them out in the long rows. They would wilt in the heat that day, but by the next morning, usually, they would be sticking up again, pert and green and orderly, in the dew-darkened ground. Each night when we quit, Jake would say to me, fairly singing: "We're getting it done, Andy boy! We're leaving it behind!"

At the end of the day, my father would come to take me home. If we were working late, which we almost always did, he would drive back to where we were. If the ground was too wet for him to drive in the fields, he would stop at the barn and blow the horn, and I would quit and hurry to meet him.

As we got near the end of the tobacco setting and Jake's elation grew, he stepped the pace up on Col and Lillybelle a little dangerously, enjoying their complaints, his own silence deepening in response. And then one night he made an invention that he liked so well that he would tell about it for years afterwards. We were working late. It was well after sundown and everybody was tired. Nearing the end of a round, Jake said, "One more round, and then . . ."

As he came to the end of the next round, he said, "One more, and then . . ."

At the end of the next he said it again.

Col, unable to stand it any longer, said, "And then *what*, old man?"

His voice dancing on laughter, the trap sprung at last, Jake said, "And *then* do another'n."

That couldn't last, of course. It all blew up in a big fracas right before dinner the next day. We could hear it clear to the plantbeds: Col making a profane speech on the theme of insurrection, Lillybelle swearing and crying, Jake protesting in the voice of surprised reason: "Well, *I* didn't know you was upset. Why didn't you all *say* something?"

Too much had been said by then to permit things to be put back the way they had been. After dinner Jake told Lillybelle to stay at the house. He drafted Ester out of the kitchen, put her on the setter with Leaf, and sent Col to the plantbed with Reenie and me.

I was sorry to have Col at the plantbed, for I had been having a good time talking with Reenie. She was curious, I think, as to what manner of creature I might be, and she drew me out by soliciting my opinions. I was full of strong opinions, which became even stronger when I discovered that they amused her, and even inspired her sometimes to agree. She liked strong opinions. In return, she told me at length about herself. She was living with her mother and her two sisters, Trill and Juanita. Juanita was the oldest, and was engaged to a goofy old boy named Calvin Sweetswing, a match that

Reenie looked down upon from a great height: "She's going to *marry* that bug-eyed silly thing! I wouldn't sweep under his lazy feet for him and ten like him!" But she seemed to dismiss the matter, nevertheless, with a sort of approval: "Well, anyhow, it keeps her out of *my* hair." Trill was another matter. Trill was only a year older than Reenie, and pretty too, as Reenie was willing to admit, and her taste in young men was very close to Reenie's. In fact, it was not unusual for them to like the same young man, and then they did not get along. Reenie was beginning to be uneasy about being so long away from home. She reminded me frequently that she did not know what Trill might be up to.

"Do you like R. T.?" I asked her.

"*That* silly thing?" She stuck out her tongue and laughed. I laughed too, in eager disloyalty to R. T.

Being Reenie's confidant there in the plantbed was a fine pleasure, surprisingly satisfying, and I hated to give it up. I had to, of course, when Jake sent Col to work with us. Col clearly knew how to talk to beautiful young women better than I did. He knew just what to say, and just how to say it. Some of his opinions were even stronger than mine, and Reenie was even gladder to agree with them. They talked, facing one another across the bed, and I listened, admiring Reenie from afar. Grudgingly, I admired Col too. He did have his ways. If Reenie had not been there, I knew, he would have been killing time—making smokes, adjusting his hat, changing places, getting up to do little jobs that did not need to be done, groaning about the pain it gave him to work in a stoop, looking off at the horizon for any help that might be coming down from the sky—Mr. Noah Count himself. But with Reenie there he worked quickly and well, putting grace into it, paying attention to what he was doing, and talking to her all the time, as if absentmindedly, as if she might be just anybody else. I would have given anything to be able to talk to her that way. He had style. His cuffs were turned back from his wrists as if to keep them from getting dirty, his hat was tilted over just right, and he had a matchstick pinched between his front teeth. I couldn't figure *how* that matchstick worked, but it worked; it was the master touch.

Knowing that Col was there with Reenie made R. T. desperate. He would hurry off to take a new supply of plants to the people in the field, or get a load of water from the pond, and then hurry back and stay until Jake hollered to him to get the hell on over there with more plants. He would load the sled then and, with a lot of backward looks, hurry away again.

The weather turned fine, and after the blowup between Col and Jake, the work went smoothly. It got to be Friday afternoon, and we were going to try to finish up by Saturday night. Col and Reenie and R. T. and I were at the plantbed. Jake hollered for water, and R. T. left to bring a new load from the pond. As soon as he was gone, Col's and Reenie's way of talking to each other changed a little, as it had begun to do. It was not a big change, but when R. T. was out of the way they spoke as people do when they are alone. For all the attention they paid to me, I might as well have been a spirit.

Reenie got up and carried an armload of plants to a basket a little way up the bed and put them in it, and then returned to her place and stood with her hands on her hips, resting. I can see her now, across all the years, as plainly as if I were still looking up at her across only the plantbed. She wore a cotton dress, red with a pattern of tiny white and yellow flowers, full-skirted, tight in the bodice. She had rings on her fingers, silver bracelets on her wrists. She had taken off her shoes. The sun behind her, her hair was all a tangle of red lights. She gave you the nice warming impression that you get from certain women, at a certain brief time in their lives, that she perfectly filled her skin: there was nothing wanting anywhere, and nothing wasted. And then, without any invitation whatsoever, my mind informed me how excellent it would be to kiss her.

She gathered her skirt and lifted it a little as she knelt and went to work again. "I'm going to go home," she said. "If Daddy won't take me, I'm going to get a ride with Wheeler."

Col looked up at her quickly and studied her, but she was looking down.

"Tomorrow will be Saturday," she said. "I got to be home by dinnertime tomorrow."

"Aw," Col said, drawing the words out gently as if speaking to a child, "you don't want to go home *yet*."

"Oh, yes I do. I'm worried about Trill. I'm scared she'll get something I won't."

Col was kneeling there across from her, his right hand holding a plant still rooted in the bed. But he had stopped. He had not pulled the plant. Perhaps he never did. He said, "Maybe you'll get something *she* won't."

While they looked at each other, time stopped. Or I suppose it did, for it is a moment that has not stopped happening, at least in *my* mind, and whatever happened next never got into my mind at all. I knew that something powerful had passed, something strange to me, as from another world, and yet pertaining to all that I had ever known in this one.

I was not exactly transfixed, for I must have kept working, but it seems to me that nothing happened at all until R. T. pulled up beside the plantbed and said, "Whoa!" He was silent a moment, looking, standing on the sled with the lines in his hands, and then he said, "Where'd Col and Reenie go?"

I looked then, and they were gone. "I don't know."

He leapt off the sled then and started to run. I got up and pitched my handful of plants into a basket and started after him.

It was one of those brilliant late spring afternoons that make things look both substantial and translucent as if made of light. The sun had got down into the last quarter of the day, and the light was stretching out across the hollows and ridges and woodlands of the farm. Jake's mules drew the setter across the patch slowly, as if its lengthening shadow made a friction on the ground, but all the rest was light. It gleams in my memory now, leaf and cloud, thicket and grassy ridge, as luminous almost as the great blue sky itself.

R. T. was running, it seemed to me, as fast as a horse, down off the ridge where the plantbeds were, on a long slant toward the woods in the hollow, and I did not catch up with him until he got in among the trees, where he had to slow down. By then it had come to me what we were running for: Col and Reenie had gone off to jigjig, though it came to me at the same time that jigjig was not the right name for it. Nor was any other word I knew. They had gone beyond all our words, somewhere beyond anywhere we knew. R. T. knew it as certainly as I did, I think, and that was why he was running so nearly out of his head. What he planned to do if he found them, I do not know. I doubt that he knew.

We sped over the ground like two young hawks. We looked into wooded hollows where the sunlight slanted in long girders, and little encampments of mayapples stood green and perfect among the heavy trunks. We searched the dry trashy floors of locust thickets. We looked into leafy rooms under the low drooping branches of sugar maples. We looked, as we leapt over them, into grassy coverts and nests in the pasture draws. We hunted over the whole farm, and though we did not find Reenie and Col in any of its receptive and secret places, all of them, the whole country, came alive for me with a possibility that I had not thought of before and have not ceased to think of since, beyond all the words that I have learned.

It wore us out finally. We gave up and started for the house, walking slow, upset because we could hear Jake calling R. T., who had not done his chores. We knew that R. T. was going to catch it. It was way after sundown, a star or two was shining, and we could smell the damp coming up out of the hollows.

I heard my father's horn. He had come to take me home, and suddenly I felt farther away than I had ever been. I stood still in the path as a shiver started in the roots of my hair and shook me.

It Wasn't Me

(*1953*)

The crowd in the courthouse square in Hargrave has not begun to assemble yet. The various pieces of it are now present, but scattered about: half a dozen bidders or potential bidders, a few who have come out of concern or interest or curiosity, a few who are on hand simply for whatever may happen, as if in loyalty to the present tense of the county's history. Wheeler Catlett has been studying the scene below him now for some minutes, its several components as telling to him as sentences written in his own hand. He stands motionless at the window, the room behind him as thoroughly forgotten as if he is not in it. He has been preparing himself for weeks for what is about to happen. And yet, since what is about to happen is still, so far as he can tell, unpredictable, he is not ready.

On the least busy side of the square Elton and Mary Penn are sitting in their car, watching the courthouse door, not moving, not talking. Their car is an old Dodge coupe, black under the dust; along the side that Wheeler can see there is an elongated fan of dried mud. On the opposite side of the square, Clara and Gladston Pettit are standing on the sidewalk with their lawyer. The three of them have not moved beyond the pale blue aura of Glad's burnished Cadillac. Talking, they stand close together as if aware of their difference from everything else in sight. Clara is wearing a fur coat and hat and gloves. Glad has on a pearl-gray overcoat and hat. The lawyer, a man much younger than Glad, coatless as if by misunderstanding of the weather, stands with his hands in his pockets, his shoulders hunched, looking curiously around him as he listens to Clara who, Wheeler imagines, is telling him that this was a familiar place to her in her girlhood. And he can imagine her tone of disparagement: "Well, *we* thought it quite a city. We were, you know, so *far* from everything." No one would know from looking at her that Clara ever rode into Hargrave behind a team of mules. She looks like a stranger—which, Wheeler guesses, is how she means to look. But from his window he can see too, beyond the cornices along Front Street, the wide slow-flowing river reaching westward, making its great difference that, as always, consoles him for lesser ones. Now the wind has roughened it, and under the brilliant sky its surface blinks with whitecaps.

Wheeler watches the triad of the two Pettits and their lawyer with distaste, but mainly out of curiosity now, for they are no longer the problem. The problem is now in the intentions and the eligibility of certain would-be buyers of a certain farm in whose fate Wheeler is urgently involved. And he is involved, now, as the agent of a dead man.

Clara Pettit's father, Old Jack Beechum, was Wheeler's client, his kinsman by marriage, and his friend. Old Jack was one of that venerable school of farmers and stockmen whose life was regulated by the knowledge of what "a good one" was and meant. Horses, mules, cattle, sheep, hogs, and people all submitted in his mind to the measure of that height of excellence represented by the known, proved, and remembered good ones of their respective kinds. Old Jack knew a good one when he saw one, and Elton Penn was a good one, and so was Mary, Elton's wife.

The Penns moved to Old Jack's farm as his tenants at the time Old Jack finally gave up his lonely independence and moved to a room in the hotel in Port William, eight years before he died. The Penns proved satisfactory. They proved, in fact, far more than satisfactory. They were good, they were Old Jack's kind, they listened to him and cared about him, they were the chief pleasure of his final years. Old Jack wanted them to have the farm after his death—and wanted the farm to have them after his death—and to that purpose he willed them what he thought would be half the purchase price.

As Wheeler told Elton on the afternoon Old Jack was buried, Old Jack also *set* the purchase price. But he did not do that in his will. He should have done so, but he did not. At that time he had hesitated to state so finally and formally what he knew: that Clara cared nothing for the place and would sell it as soon as it was hers. The father and daughter were irreconcilably different, irreconcilably divided, and yet he loved her, and he was torn. So he left the farm to Clara and the empowering sum of money to Elton and Mary. He set the price several years later in a letter to Wheeler in the little notebook that he kept in the bib pocket of his overalls, where they found it after he died. By the time he wrote the note, Old Jack was often absent from himself; he apparently wrote it in some passing moment of realization and anxiety, and then forgot it—for how long before he died, Wheeler does not know. The note, the pencil scrawl trenched deeply into the tiny page, read:

> Wheeler see the
> boy has his place
> 200 $ acre be
> about right she
> ought to not
> complain Wheeler
> see to it

The slow, crooked legend of that page fell upon Wheeler's conscience with a palpable gravity, as if the old man had reached out from beyond the grave and laid a hand on him. The letter, of course, was of no legal worth whatsoever. In the eyes of a court it would answer no pertinent question. Who was "the boy"? What was "his place"? Who was "Wheeler"? Who, for that matter, wrote the letter? But Wheeler, had he been the one to be held, would have been held tighter by that letter, that outcry, than by the will itself. He himself had no question as to the intention or the authenticity of the letter, and he assumed that Clara, understanding what was obviously her father's dying wish, would be bound by it as a matter of course.

He was mistaken. He had done his assuming, as he often did, in a world that he assumed was ruled by instinctive decency. That Clara and Glad Pettit did not inhabit that particular world, they let him know fast. After the reading of Old Jack's will, Wheeler asked them to remain in his office to speak privately with him. He thereupon showed them the letter in the notebook, explained what it meant, and suggested that they proceed with the sale of the farm to Elton and Mary Penn at the stipulated price.

Clara quickly glanced at her husband in a way that alone ought to have informed Wheeler that he had driven his ducks to the wrong pond.

"No," Glad Pettit said.

And then Clara herself said, "No."

That was not a reply calculated to please Wheeler, and it certainly did not. It surprised him too. He was surprised at Clara, and surprised at the extent of his own innocence, which had left him now without a plan. He had begun the conversation leaning back in his chair; now he sat forward, lacing his fingers in front of him. Making an effort to suppress his irritation, he said, "Excuse me, Clara, but are you sure you understand the reasons for what I just proposed?"

"Yes," she said, looking at Glad and then back at Wheeler. "I understand. Of course I do."

Wheeler studied her—a plumpish lady, now beyond her middle years, opulently dressed, her perfectly manicured hands resting on her purse in her lap. She was wearing a smart little pillbox hat with a veil, and behind the veil her eyes were looking straight at Wheeler. She did understand. She knew exactly what she was doing. And yet he was not ready to give up.

"Surely you can't feel that you're being deceived. The letter there in the notebook—no court would honor it, of course, but among us there can be no doubt."

"I have no doubt."

"And this is a most deserving young couple. I don't have to tell you how well and honorably they've taken care of the place, and how kindly and hospitably they treated your father."

Seeing the embarrassment that Wheeler intended for Clara, Gladston Pettit stepped in. "Wheeler, you as a lawyer and I as a banker know that this is purely a matter of law—of principle, I would say. The kindness of this young couple was undoubtedly great. We don't question it. They have our gratitude. But their kindness was not to Clara, it was to her father, and it has been amply, some would say extravagantly, repaid. As for their farming, it was done in fulfillment of their half of a contract, of which the other half was also well and honorably fulfilled. All Clara is asking for, Wheeler, is what is rightly hers. She has the right to fair market value for her property."

Glad's voice had an unction in it that implied what he scrupled to say: that poor Clara would not, in fact, receive fair market value for her property, because her father's too-generous bequest to the Penns must be seen as, in effect, a deduction from that value. And his tone conveyed as well the implicit accusation that Wheeler, as Old Jack's lawyer, being obviously of sounder mind, should have counseled him against such overgenerosity. Neither the speech nor any of its implications suited Wheeler, who never had liked Glad's way of reducing things to their barest (usually monetary) essentials—his habitual reduction of principle to his own interest—and he disliked too to be put in the position, an odd one for a lawyer, of both knowing and resenting Clara's rights.

He knew, anyhow, that he was licked, and in spite of himself his exasperation had begun to show. While Glad talked, Wheeler had regarded him with a look suggestive that human discourse had not been expectable from that quarter. And then he swiveled his chair away from Glad in a movement that seemed not merely to dismiss him but to forget him as well. He made himself smile and addressed his final plea to Clara:

"It's not a question of what was owed and what was paid, Clara. That wasn't what Uncle Jack had on his mind. There were other questions that he put ahead of that one. What would be best for this good pair of young people? What would be best for this good farm? What should be done here for the good of the world?—Uncle Jack would have put it that way, and I hope you don't mind if I do. He thought it over a lot of times, and he concluded that the best thing would be to put the good people and the good farm together—to bind their fates together, so to speak. I know he thought about it that way. I heard him talk about it that way. It's not an old man's senile foolishness. He knew what he was doing." He paused, look-ing at Clara, and then he said, "Clara, I don't know anybody more worthy to walk in your daddy's tracks than Elton Penn. And your daddy loved him."

And that failed too, for Clara said, "My father's loves are not mine."

After that, the Pettits communicated with Wheeler by way of a Louisville lawyer, and they had little enough to communicate. Old association, family ties, the dead man's wishes were left to blow as the wind listed. But Old Jack's letter, failing to hold Clara, held Wheeler. His duties as executor of Old Jack's will were soon ful-filled, but disemployment brought him none of the benefits of the disemployed. There was no rest in it for him, no possibility that he and the problem of the dishonored letter might leave one another alone. The farm, according to the Pettits' wishes, was to be sold at the courthouse door early in January, and until that day had passed the problem was Wheeler's as much as it was Elton and Mary Penn's. It was not a problem appointed to him, but one that he in-herited, a part of his own legacy from his deceased client and friend. Jack Beechum came back to haunt him, and often in the small hours of the night Wheeler would find himself talking and arguing with the old man face to face. Trying to end these encounters, he would cry out in his thoughts: "But I *did* try! I can't, damn it, *make* 'em do it!" And then he would think, no longer arguing but only mourn-ing, that the Pettits were playing a different game from any that Old Jack had every played, and living in a different world from the one that he had lived in. The letter in the notebook was written in a lan-guage the Pettits did not speak; they had forgot the tongue in which an old man might cry out from his grave in love and in defense of a possibility no longer his own in this world.

But it was not merely that the old man would not take no for an answer; Wheeler could not bring himself to offer it for an answer. The truth is that Wheeler is a seer of visions—not the heavenly visions of saints and mystics, but the earthly ones of a mainly practical man who sees the good that has been possible in this world, and, beyond that, the good that is desirable in it. Wheeler has known the hundred and fifty acres called, until now, the Beechum place all his life. It is a good farm, a third or so of it rough enough, but the rest of it plenty good, and all of it well cared for for a long time. It is a pretty place too. The fences and buildings have been kept up. The yard in front of the old house is full of low-spreading maples. And behind the house there is an ample garden plot with a grape arbor and a dozen old pear and apple trees. It is a place with good human life already begun in it, where the right sort of young man and woman could do well. Knowing all this, knowing the farm, knowing Elton and Mary Penn, Wheeler has irresistibly imagined the life they might live there. He does not think of it, of course, as the life they *will* live there, for he is aware of chance and human nature and mortality, but it is a life that they could hope to live, and a life that, Wheeler believes, a certain number of people in every generation *must* hope to live and try to live. He wants Elton and Mary to have that hope and make that effort there on Old Jack's place where they have, in fact, already begun. And so Wheeler has a reason of his own not to take no for an answer.

Though the direct way was now lost, and the only available route appeared to wander in thicket and hollow without a plan, he would not give up. He did not give up when he learned for certain that there would be one strong contending bidder, nor when he learned that there would be at least two. He did not know what could be done, but he did not give up. And he found it necessary to exercise his stubbornness on Elton's behalf as well as his own.

In addition to the good judgment and good sense that Old Jack and Wheeler have admired in him, Elton has pride enough to overpower sense and judgment both—such pride that, as Wheeler understands, puts him more in need of a friend than it will let him admit. Being Old Jack's heir was a nervous business for Elton in the first place. Nothing in his experience had prepared him for a benefit that was unasked, unearned, and unexpected. Nothing in his character prepared him to be comfortable with an obligation he could not repay. His election, both public and unexpected, to sonship to a man already dead took more getting used to than he'd had time for when he learned of the opposition between himself and the other heir.

His impulse, on hearing of that, was to declare his own independence at any cost, to renounce his share in Old Jack's estate along with whatever chance he had to buy the farm, and simply walk off, flinging defiance behind him like a handful of ashes.

"Whoa!" Wheeler said. "Wait a minute, now."

And Mary said, "Oh, Elton!"

Wheeler was standing with his hat and raincoat on in the middle of the kitchen floor, having just told them the outcome of his discussion with the Pettits. When he entered in response to their call, Elton and Mary had just sat down to supper. Though he had expected it, Wheeler was distressed by the intensity of Elton's embarrassment.

"Wait, Elton," he said. "You can't do that."

"Well, I'd like to know why in the hell I can't!"

Wheeler went to the table then and pulled out a chair and sat down.

"Here, Wheeler," Mary said, starting to get up. "Let me get you a plate."

"No. Don't, Mary. I have to go home."

But he sat on with them while they ate, patiently explaining—

though he knew that Elton knew—that there could now be no backing out. To go ahead was best in Elton's own interest, best in Mary's interest, best in the interest of any children they might have.

"You've got to try for it, Elton," Mary said.

"That's right," Wheeler said. "You're in a fix, I admit, that I didn't want to see you in, and didn't think you'd be in. I know it won't be easy for you to try for it and lose it. And you could do that. But you could come out with the farm too."

He hushed and sat with his head down, looking at his hands at rest on his lap, thinking. Elton and Mary sat watching him, no longer eating. And then Wheeler raised his head and looked at them. "Listen," he said. "Think about Jack Beechum getting his start here—way back yonder, seventy or seventy-five years ago. He was young and strong, excited by what he could do, demanding a lot of himself and of the place. And some things he asked were wrong. You've heard him tell it. He made mistakes that damaged him and the farm too, and that delayed and hampered him a long time. But he had the grace and the intelligence to learn and to keep on. And Ben Feltner, who was, you know, his brother-in-law, but a second father to him too, stood by him and put in a word when it would help, and helped in other ways.

"And those years changed him. He learned to do what his place asked of him. He became the man it asked him to be. He knew what it had cost him to become that kind of farmer, he knew he'd become his farm's belonging, necessary to it, and he knew he was getting old.

"He was getting old, and he had no successor. He had an heir, but no successor. As his own workdays were coming to an end, he saw his farm going into a kind of widowhood. He'd talk about it sometimes.

"And then you and Mary came along. He saw right away what the two of you and the old farm could mean to each other, and what you meant to him. He saw that you could be the man and woman the place was asking for, and his life's work might not go to waste, after all."

"We've got to try it for Mr. Beechum's sake, Elton."

"Well," Elton said, and cleared his throat. "Well, of course, *that's* why we've got to try."

Wheeler sat on with them for a while, talking of other things. When he got up to go he laid his hand on Elton's shoulder and said, "Don't worry." He knew it was useless to say that to Elton, but he meant it. His own determination had grown, for he was in the presence of what he desired. "I don't know what we'll do, but we'll do something."

That there was plenty to worry about was soon evident. Earl Benson, who lived on one of the farms adjoining the Beechum place, had bought two neighboring farms, the first of which joined his own original farm, the second being divided from it by the Beechum place. It was a pattern that did not leave much to guess. Earl Benson was expected to be a bidder, and gossip soon confirmed that he would be. Wheeler knew the man, had done legal work for him in fact, and liked him. But meeting him on the street one afternoon, he said to him: "Earl, if Elton Penn can buy the Beechum place, and he wants to, you'll have a good neighbor."

To which Earl replied, around his cigar, pleasantly enough: "And if *I* buy it, I'll have a good farm."

That didn't surprise Elton any more than it did Wheeler.

"I figured that," Elton said. "If I was in his place, I reckon I'd try to buy it too."

Wheeler was sitting in his car with the motor running, Elton leaning down to talk to him through the window. A few feet away Elton's tractor was standing with its motor running.

Wheeler had begun to make these visits almost daily, not because he had news for Elton that often, but because he was anxious and could not stay away. Wheeler's own farm was close by, and so it was easy for him, when he went there, to stop by to see Elton.

"With Earl in it," Wheeler said, "you'll have to bid higher than you want to. You might as well get ready for that."

"I'm ready to go a little bit higher."

Wheeler thought it would have to be more than a little bit, but he didn't say so. He said, "Well, I'll see you."

Two days later, Wheeler was stopped in the post office by Dr. Stedman.

"Just the man I want to see," the doctor said, taking hold of Wheeler's elbow.

"Wheeler," he said in the low, confidential voice with which some people talk to lawyers about serious matters, "I've got a little backlog of cash that I'm thinking of investing in land."

"Well, do it," Wheeler said. He was in a hurry, and he was impatient anyhow with the doctor's persistent raids on him for free advice, legal and other.

When the doctor starts with his questions, Wheeler always wants to say, "While we're standing here, Doc, would you mind taking my pulse?" But so far he has never said it. He merely saves himself as much time and trouble as possible by discovering what the doctor wants to do and advising him forthwith to do it. Even so, he always has to suffer an explanation.

"Well now," the doctor said, "that old Beechum place up by Port William, I hear it's going to be sold at auction."

"That's right."

"I hear it's a good one."

"Yessir. It's a good one." There was more, Wheeler knew, and he did not want to hear it. He shifted his weight to turn away, but the grip on his elbow tightened.

"That young fellow who lives there, Elton Penn, I understand he made the old man a good tenant."

"That's right."

"Well," the doctor said, pursing his lips, looking down and looking up, "my thinking is this. If I bought the farm, he'd make *me* a good tenant. With my obligations, you know, I'd need somebody there who wouldn't require a lot of seeing to. Do you see what I mean?"

"I do."

"So if I could get the place and a good man on it at the same time, it would solve my problems, don't you see? It would kill two birds with one stone."

Wheeler knew very well the history of those two birds, the wish to own land, and the wish to have somebody else worry about it, and there were certain things that he was prepared to say on the subject. But he gently freed his elbow, and just as gently took hold of the doctor's arm. "Doctor, do you know that Elton Penn wants to buy that farm for himself?"

"No, sir, I didn't."

"Well, he does. Listen. If you want to do a public service, get out of his way and let him have it."

Wheeler turned away then, leaving the doctor's reply floating in the air.

And so there was another bad possibility to warn Elton about.

"I don't know how far he'll go," Wheeler said, "I don't know how much money he's got."

"More than I got," Elton said.

That Elton himself made the farm attractive to at least one of his competitors, Wheeler decided not to tell him.

Standing at the window, looking down, Wheeler thinks again, as he has many times, of the terms of a possible surrender. If the farm goes too high, why should Elton not just let it go? He would have his money still. He could take his time and find another place to buy— one that maybe, in the long run, would suit him just as well. And that was all right, as far as it went. But it left out Old Jack. It left the letter in the little notebook unanswered. It failed to answer Old Jack's, and Wheeler's, notion of what the farm itself needed and deserved. The living man no more than the dead one could bear to see the little farm's boundaries dissolved in Earl Benson's adding of house to house and field to field. And if the doctor bought it? Wheeler knows that story as well as if it had already happened. Elton would not stay, and the doctor was right in supposing that he needed Elton along with the farm. He needed somebody who knew how to farm it, for he did not know how to farm it himself. When Elton and Mary left, they would be followed by a procession of other tenants who would also leave, worse following worse, while the farm ran down.

"No," Wheeler says. "Hell, no."

The sound of his own voice seems to move him. He glances at the clock on the courthouse tower, and then looks at his watch. He turns, walks slowly, looking at the floor, to the hat rack in the corner of the room, puts on his hat and coat, and returns to the window.

Clara is talking animatedly with Gladston and the lawyer, her coat collar turned up against the wind. As he watches her, it seems to Wheeler that she is elated, and he realizes with the sudden astonishment that one feels in looking into a life beyond the possibilities of one's own, that for her the sale of the farm is a freedom, her own connection with it, her own early life there, being merely an encumbrance, probably an embarrassment. This whole passage of time has been burdened for Wheeler by his dislike of the Pettits, and he feels it now. He feels it, exults in it a little, for he knows that it defines his true allegiance, and yet is sorry for it. How much better it would be to be at peace with them, fellow mortals as they are, kindred as they are. And yet he feels, as he knows Old Jack felt, the irreconcilable division between his kind and their kind, between the things of this world and their value in money.

Now the courthouse door opens. The auctioneer crosses the porch, takes his stand at the top of the steps, begins to summon the crowd. Buttoning his coat, Wheeler hurriedly crosses the room and goes out. "Back in a minute," he says to Miss Hallie, his secretary, as he strides through the outer office. She widens her eyes by way of comment as the door slams and his steps quicken going down the stairs.

Outside, the unblemished winter sunlight and the strong wind fill the square. Wheeler comes out into it with a relief and a pleasure that are familiar to him. This is the sort of day that makes an active man working inside feel that he is missing something. The year is starting. The weather is busy. Out over the river he sees a flock of birds fly up into the face of the wind and then turn, as one, away from it.

Once he is in the street, with the square in sight again, he slows down, looking, pausing, speaking to passersby as he makes his way toward the little crowd collecting at the foot of the courthouse steps. He lets the crowd shape itself before he gets there, and then he stops on its outer edge.

The crowd is hollow-centered, a kind of diffidence making everybody stay back a little, not wanting to appear too interested. The

Penns are standing in front of Wheeler on the inside of the ring. Wheeler sees Mary looking around for him. He catches her eye, gives her a quick nod. She whispers to Elton then, her lips forming the words: "Wheeler's here." Elton nods, but does not look back. Mary is holding to Elton's arm, huddled against him, more from nervousness, Wheeler knows, than from the chill in the wind. There is something in the set of Elton's head and shoulders that denies the crowd and sets him aside from it even though he is in it.

Dr. Stedman is standing close to the foot of the steps. He looks away when Wheeler looks at him, and carefully does not look back. And then Wheeler catches Earl Benson's eye and nods, and Earl throws his head back, grinning on both sides of his cigar, and gives him a wave. The Pettits and their lawyer have moved closer to the crowd. They see Wheeler and nod, and he tips his hat. Though the day is brilliant and the sun in sheltered places gives some warmth, in the open square the wind presses upon them with an irresistible chill; people stand with their hands in their pockets and their shoulders hunched.

The auctioneer gives a little introductory speech, welcoming everybody, describing the property to be sold, explaining the terms of the sale. And then, starting into his spiel, he calls for a bid of $175 an acre. The figure is hardly named before Wheeler sees Elton nod.

"Well, that's aggressive enough," Wheeler thinks. He would have been a little slower than that himself, maybe, but he sees that Elton is performing in the way proper to him, and he is pleased. "Be careful, now," he thinks.

The doctor gives a little wave of his hand at $200, and at $225 Earl Benson says loudly, "Yeah!" And so they've gone beyond Old Jack's price at a run. The auctioneer asks for $250.

"Two thirty-five," Elton says, slowing it down, and Wheeler thinks, "That's right."

Earl Benson comes in quickly at $245. The spiel continues for some time after that without a bid. Elton and Mary are talking in whispers. The doctor shakes his head, turns away, and then changes his mind and bids again: $255. Earl Benson bids $265 as quickly as before. The doctor, finished, puts his hand back in his pocket and sidles into the crowd.

Wheeler is watching only Elton now, but Elton is shaking his head at Mary, ready to quit. And then, making one of the sudden shifts from stillness to haste that is characteristic of him, Wheeler steps through the crowd just as Elton is turning away and the auctioneer's hand is raised in the air. He stops at Elton's left shoulder, a little behind him, and takes hold of his arm. He says, "Go on!" and when Elton hesitates, "It'll be all *right*! Go on!" And Wheeler knows, he can feel in his hand, when Elton yields himself to his struggle again—can feel him settling onto his feet.

"Two seventy-five," Elton says.

The auctioneer looks at Earl Benson. His tone has grown quiet now and personal, the public auction reduced to a conversation among three men. He is asking Earl if he will pay $285.

For a long time Earl does not give any sign that he knows he is where he is. He is looking down, thinking, and Wheeler knows within a guess or two what he is thinking about. He has a mortgage against his home place. He has the bank to account to. He has interest and wages to pay. He has bills for fuel and fertilizer and seed and parts and supplies. He has something to gain, and perhaps more to lose. He stands with his head down while desire and pride argue with chance, mortality, and arithmetic. Finally he raises his head, looks at the auctioneer, looks away, and nods.

Before the auctioneer can begin his spiel again, Wheeler's hand has tightened on Elton's arm and Elton has said, "Two ninety."

"That's right," Wheeler says.

And there is another pause, and Earl Benson bids $295.

"Go on," Wheeler says, and Elton says, "Three hundred."

They wait then while the auctioneer speaks to Earl, who shakes his head once, and again, and turns away.

The auctioneer brings his hand down. "Sold! To Elton Penn here, for three hundred dollars an acre."

Elton, shaken, still shaking, looks at Wheeler and grins. "Is that me?"

And the auctioneer, overhearing, laughs and says, "You Elton Penn, ain't you, honey?"

Wheeler leaves Elton and Mary to complete their purchase, and goes back to his office. In the privacy of the dark stairway, he allows himself to grin at last, in relief and triumph, and in his mind he says to Old Jack, "How's *that*?" And to himself he says, "And what's next?" He pretty well knows what is next. He is still hurrying.

He shuts his office door and, without taking off his overcoat and hat, picks up a yellow pad with some figures on it, reads them over, and then sits down and rapidly works his way through another set of figures.

Elton and Mary have paid a hundred dollars an acre more than the two hundred stipulated by Old Jack's letter. And so Clara's dishonoring of that letter has earned her, and cost the Penns, $15,000. The place has cost $45,000, of which Old Jack's legacy to the Penns will cover a third, and Wheeler assumes that they will have savings that will increase that by somewhat. By Wheeler's own estimate, the farm would have been worth its price to anybody at $250 an acre, which puts Elton above the mark by $7,500. Going beyond $250, Wheeler thought beforehand and still thinks, might be justifiable for Earl Benson, who owns adjoining land, or for Elton, whose occupation of the place and whose familiarity with it, both from his own experience and Old Jack's instruction, would have a practical worth. Whether or not that worth would reach $7,500, Wheeler does not know. But at that point he would, anyhow, shift the ground of justification: Elton and Mary ought to have the farm because they are worthy of it.

Studying his figures, considering all that he knows to consider, Wheeler concludes that the Penns are safe enough. Assuming that they can continue to do as well as they have done, they will own their farm—which is perhaps as good a chance as anybody could ask.

But Wheeler is not done assuming yet. If he assumes, as he must, that if left alone Elton would have stopped bidding at $235, then Wheeler must consider himself in some manner responsible for $9,750 of the Penns' debt. He cannot come up with that kind of money without selling something that he ought to keep, and he does not need it now, anyway; he may not need it ever, but he knows that he must regard it as one of the possible prices of his own freedom.

He does another brief computation, and picks up the telephone. He calls the cashier of the Hargrave Farmers' Bank and finds that he can spare a thousand dollars, and he arranges for the transfer of that sum to a savings account in the name of Beechum, Catlett, and Penn. "I'll send the check right over," he says. "Yes. That's right. That's the name of the company." He hangs up, takes a check pad from the drawer of his desk, writes out a check, and seals it in an envelope.

He has been sitting upright on the edge of his chair, and now he leans back, pushes his hat off his forehead, and lapses into stillness. But even still, he remains expectant, listening, and soon he hears the street door open and shut and then footsteps coming up the stairs.

Miss Hallie opens the door. "Elton Penn is here."

"Tell him to come in," Wheeler says, and then, himself, calls, "Come in, Elton." As Miss Hallie goes out, he hands her the envelope. "Take that to the bank, please."

When Elton comes in, Wheeler grins at him. "Well. You've come out all right, I think."

"I don't know, Wheeler. I might have made one hell of a mistake." Elton is as tightly strung as a banjo, and there is a little glistening in his eyes.

"Sit down," Wheeler says, and Elton does.

"Where's Mary?"

"The grocery store," Elton says. That is not what he has come to talk about.

"Well, it could have been better," Wheeler says. "No doubt about that." And then he grins again and says, "And it could have been worse."

"This was bad enough, maybe. What do you think?"

"I think it was a shame it had to happen the way it did. A damned shame. I don't understand—" Wheeler stops then and shakes his head. "But I suppose we mustn't say everything we think."

He picks up the pad with his figures on it and looks at it, thinking, for a minute, and then pitches it back onto the desk. "I know you're worried about the price, Elton. But it's an amount I think you can manage—if you live, of course, and stay on your feet."

"I could get sick or die too," Elton says.

Wheeler laughs. "Of course you could. But I don't see how we can depend on that. I'm afraid we'll just have to assume that you won't. It's a risky business." He swivels his chair toward the window and looks at the sky a moment, recovering his thought, and then turns back to Elton. "In other words, I think you did what you should have done. You have the farm, and I believe you're going to be glad of it. And *I'm* glad of it. It's a great relief to me."

"Well, of course, if I'd lost it, I'd have been sick. But I can still lose it."

"No, my boy. You're not going to lose it. Not if we *both* can help it. I told you to go ahead because it would be all right. You must understand that I meant that. If you need help, I'm going to help you."

"But, damn it, Wheeler, don't you think I *ought* to lose it if I can't make it on my own?"

"No," Wheeler says. "I *don't* think that. I can see how a person *might* think that. It seems to me I thought something like that myself once. But I don't think it anymore."

"It's the obligation, Wheeler." Elton looks up at Wheeler and his eyes glisten again. "If it hadn't been for you, Wheeler, I'd have lost that farm today. I know it, and I appreciate it. But why should you have done that? Why should you have felt obliged to help me get into a problem that now you feel obliged to help me get out of?"

Wheeler knows this longing for independence in Elton because he knows it in himself. He knows that he is a trespasser, and he feels suddenly heavy with the complexity and difficulty of what he has begun. But he is amused too and is trying not to show it. Like any young man who has won his heart's desire, Elton wishes he had won it by himself, wishes to possess it on his own terms, its first and only lover.

"It wasn't me," Wheeler says, and is at once startled by his words and filled with a sort of glee by them. "It wasn't me. If I had stood back and let you lose that farm, or let it lose you, that old man would have talked to me in the dark for the rest of my life."

"You did it out of loyalty to Mr. Beechum?"

"Partly." Wheeler studies the man sitting in front of him, who is sitting there studying him, puzzled by him at the moment, Wheeler guesses, and waiting courteously for him to say what he is talking about. And Wheeler again feels his great liking for this Elton Penn—a young man, as Old Jack would say, with a good head on his shoulders. An orderly man, who makes order around him.

"The place," Wheeler says, "is not its price. Its price stands for it for just a minute or two while it's bought and sold, and may hang over it a while after that and have an influence on it, but the place has been here since the evening and the morning were the third day. The figures are like us—here and gone."

"The figures make it mine," Elton says, "if I can be equal to 'em."

"The figures give you the right to call it yours for a little while."

"They give me the right to do a hell of a lot more than that."

For some time now they do not say anything. There is more feeling in what Elton has said than he has found words for, and more than Wheeler wants to deal with in a hurry. Wheeler is amused by Elton's predicament, and yet is moved and troubled by it. Here is a young man whose experience has taught him the meaning of debt, who wants above all to be paid up and in the clear, and who has become first the inheritor of a bequest that he did not ask for and did not expect, and next the beneficiary of an act of friendship that he did not ask for and, with part of his mind, does not want. Wheeler sits and looks at Elton while Elton sits and looks at the palm of his right hand, oppressed between gratitude and resentment. Watching him struggle in his confines, Wheeler realizes again the fatality of what he has undertaken. He has started something that he will have to finish. And how long will that be?

The office has faded away around them. They might as well be in a barn, or in an open field. They are meeting in the world, Wheeler thinks, striving to determine how they will continue in it. Both of them are still wearing their hats and coats.

"People have been exercising those rights here for a hundred and seventy-five years or so," he says finally, "and in general they've wasted more than they've saved. One of the rights the figures give is the right to ruin."

"You're talking about something you learned out of a book, Wheeler."

"I'm talking about something that I learned from Jack Beechum, among others, and something you'll learn too, if you stay put and pay attention, whether I tell it to you or not."

"Do you know what I want, Wheeler?"

"I expect I do. But tell me."

"I want to make it on my own. I don't want a soul to thank."

Wheeler thinks, "Too late," but he does not say it. He grins. That he knows the futility of that particular program does not prevent him from liking it. "Well," he says, "putting aside whatever Mary Penn might have to say about that, and putting aside what it means in the first place just to be a living human, I don't think your old friend has left you in shape to live thankless."

He sees that Elton sees, or is beginning to. This man who longs to be independent cannot bear to be ungrateful. Wheeler knows that. But the suffering of obligation is still on Elton, and he says, "What do you mean?"

"I mean you're a man indebted to a dead man. So am I. So was he. That's the story of it. Back of you is Jack Beechum. Back of him was Ben Feltner. Back of him was, I think, his own daddy. And back of him somebody else, and on back that way, who knows how far? And I'm back of you because Jack Beechum is, and because he's back of me, along with some others.

"It's no use to want to make it on your own, because you can't. Oh, Glad Pettit, I reckon, would say you can, but Glad Pettit deals in a kind of property you can put in your pocket. Or he thinks he does. But when you quit living in the price and start living in the place, you're in a different line of succession."

Elton laughs. "The line of succession I'm in says you've got to make it on your own. I'm in the line of succession of root, hog, or die."

"That may have been the line of succession you *were* in, but it's not the one you're in now. The one you're in now is different."

"Well, how did I get in it?" Elton says almost in a sigh, as if longing to be out of it.

"The way you got in it, I guess, was by being chosen. The way you stay in it is by choice."

"And I got in because Mr. Beechum chose me."

"And Mary. He chose you and Mary. He thought you two were a good match, and that mattered to him. His own marriage, you know, was not good. Yes. You could say he chose you. But there's more to it. He chose you, we'd have to say too, because he'd been chosen. The line is long, and not straight."

Wheeler pauses for a minute. He's leaning a little forward now, his elbows resting on the chair arms, his hands loosely joined in front of him.

"And then we'd have to say that, through him, the farm chose you."

Elton looks straight at him. "The *farm* did."

Wheeler smiles. "The land expects something from us. The line of succession, the true line, is the membership of people who know it does. Uncle Jack knew it, and he knew you would answer."

"Now wait a minute," Elton says. "Hold on."

But Wheeler sees a little of the way ahead now, and he keeps going. "We start out expecting things of it. All of us do, I think. And then some of us, if we stay put and pay attention, see that expectations are going the other way too. Demands are being made of us, whether we know it or know what they are or not. The place is crying out to us to do better, to be worthy of it. Uncle Jack knew that."

Wheeler stops again and looks at Elton. "He thought you were worthy. Do you remember that spring day when he first came to visit, after you and Mary moved in?"

"In May, 1945," Elton says. "The day Germany surrendered."

"Well, right then he started hoping that you and Mary would own the farm. He mentioned it to me that same evening. I remember it very well. I said, 'Well, what do you think of Elton Penn?' And he said, 'I think he's a good one.'"

"But, Wheeler," Elton says, and there is a catch of tenderness in his voice now, and there is some fear in it, "Maybe he was wrong about me."

"Maybe," Wheeler says. "But he didn't think so—he didn't change his mind in seven years—and *I* don't think so."

Wheeler is remembering the first time he ever saw Elton. It was the March of 1944, and Wheeler was trying to persuade Old Jack to leave his farm and take up residence in the hotel in Port William. Since his wife's death Old Jack had lived alone and had done, as he said, a good job of it. But now everybody who cared about him was worried about him. He was too old, they thought, to be living by himself, and Wheeler had begun his argument, which he soon saw would have to be improved. If Old Jack was ever to be persuaded to move out, somebody Wheeler could *vouch* for would have to be ready to move in.

Because of the war, suitable people were even less available than usual, but finally Wheeler heard of a tenant on a rough farm beyond the little crossroads of Goforth, a young fellow by the name of Elton Penn, who was looking for a better place.

When Wheeler stopped in Goforth to ask directions—it was a bright, warm, windy morning—his sometime client, Braymer Hardy, was sitting on a keg in front of the store.

Having got his directions, Wheeler asked, "What about this boy, Elton Penn, Braymer?"

"He'll do!"

"Well, what do you know about him?"

"He's been on his own ever since he was fourteen, Wheeler. He's sort of a half orphan, you might say. He's made a crop ever' year since he was fourteen, and ever' damn one of 'em's been a good one."

"Can you depend on him?"

Braymer nodded. "Yessir. You can depend on him."

Wheeler started his car.

"I'd a thought you'd a knowed this boy, Wheeler. Didn't he sprout over about Port William?"

"I don't know."

"His daddy was Albert Penn. You knowed him."

"Yes. I knew Albert. So this is Albert's boy."

"I expect Albert was dead and they was gone from over there before Elton got growed up enough for a fellow to know."

"I expect so," Wheeler said.

He followed the gravel road on down into the valley toward the farm he had been directed to, but before he reached the turnoff to the house he found his man.

Elton was plowing a field in the bottom that began level along the creek and then rose gradually up toward the steeper slope of the valley side. Wheeler saw that the plowlands were laid out correctly. He saw the quality of the thought that had gone ahead of the work, the design of the year's usage laid neatly and considerately upon the natural shape of the field. Elton was working a team of black Percherons. He had them stepping, urging them and himself, and yet there was an appearance of ease in their work that to Wheeler bespoke the accomplishment of the workman: the horses were fitted and harnessed and hitched right; the plow was running right.

Having already stopped his car, Wheeler turned off the engine, and in the quiet that followed, in which he could hear the wind, he sat and looked. Watching Elton, he might, he felt, have been watching his own father as a young man, or Old Jack himself as a young man. He realized, as he had not done before, how it had been with them. He felt himself in the presence of a rare and passionate excellence belonging to his history and his country, and he was moved. He sat there a long time, watching, forgetting the year he was in.

"Maybe we *were* wrong about you," he says to Elton. "You've still got time to prove us wrong. But it's too late now for me to believe you will."

Elton sits with his head down, thinking. The question they have come to now requires a long proof. The burden of time is on him. When he dies, somebody will answer.

And then he looks up again at Wheeler. "So this has happened now because of all these things coming together—because Mr. Beechum wanted it to happen, and because the farm, as you say, wanted it to, and because you wanted it to."

"And because you and Mary wanted it to," Wheeler says.

Elton looks at him and slowly nods.

"And because what has happened has been desirable to a lot of people we never knew, who lived before us."

Elton nods, looks down, thinks again, and again looks up. "And you're saying you're going to be my friend because of all that?"

"Yes. Because of you yourself, and because of all that."

Elton laughs. "You're going to be my friend, it sounds pret' near like, because you can't get out of it."

"If I was his friend, given what that meant, I can't get out of it."

"But, Wheeler, that's pretty tough."

"It's tough. It's not as tough as being nobody's friend."

"You're saying there's not any way to get out of this friendship."

"No. You can get out of it. By not accepting it. I'm the one, so far, who can't escape it. You have it because I've given it to you, and you don't have to accept. I gave it to you because it was given to me, and I accepted."

Elton draws a long breath, and holds it, looking out the window, and then breathes it out and looks at Wheeler. "I can't repay him, Wheeler. And now you've helped me, and I can't repay you."

"Well, that's the rest of it," Wheeler says. "It's not accountable. If the place was its price, or you thought it was, maybe you could consider such debts payable—but then some of those debts you wouldn't have contracted, and the rest you wouldn't recognize as debts. Your debt to Jack Beechum *is* a debt, and it's *not* payable—not to him, anyhow. Your debt to me is smaller than your debt to him, not much at all, and it may or may not be payable to me. This is only human friendship. I could need a friend too, you know. I could get sick or die too."

Elton says, "Well, I—"

But Wheeler raises a hand, and goes on. "It's not accountable, because we're dealing in goods and services that we didn't make, that can't exist at all except as gifts. Everything about a place that's different from its price is a gift. Everything about a man or woman that's different from their price is a gift. The life of a neighborhood is a gift. I know that if you bought a calf from Nathan Coulter you'd pay him for it, and that's right. But aside from that, you're friends and neighbors, you work together, and so there's lots of giving and taking without a price—some that you don't remember, some that you never knew about. You don't send a bill. You don't, if you can help it, keep an account. Once the account is kept and the bill presented, the friendship ends, the neighborhood is finished, and you're back to where you started. The starting place doesn't have anybody in it but you."

"It's before the line of succession," Elton says.

"That's right."

Wheeler leans back in his chair now and spreads his hands and lets them hang relaxed over the ends of the chair arms. "So." He thinks of Old Jack again, at ease with that imperious ghost at last.

He looks at Elton. "So. There is to be no repayment. Because there is to be no bill. Do you see what I mean?"

"Maybe." Elton grins, at ease now too, looking at Wheeler, his hand fishing in his shirt pocket for his cigarettes. "Probably."

Wheeler laughs. "Well, give me one of your smokes."

The Boundary

(1965)

He can hear Margaret at work in the kitchen. That she knows well what she is doing and takes comfort in it, one might tell from the sounds alone as her measured, quiet steps move about the room. It is all again as it has been during the almost twenty years that only the two of them have lived in the old house. Sitting in the split-hickory rocking chair on the back porch, Mat listens; he watches the smoke from his pipe drift up and out past the foliage of the plants in their hanging pots. He has finished his morning stint in the garden, and brought in a half-bushel of peas that he set down on the drainboard of the sink, telling Margaret, "There you are, ma'am."

He heard with pleasure her approval, "Oh! They're nice!" and then he came out onto the shady porch to rest.

Since winter he has not felt well. Through the spring, while Nathan and Elton and the others went about the work of the fields, Mat, for the first time, confined himself to the house and barn lot and yard and garden, working a little and resting a little, finding it easier than he expected to leave the worry of the rest of it to Nathan. But slowed down as he is, he has managed to make a difference. He has made the barn his business, and it is cleaner and in better order than it has been for years. And the garden, so far, is nearly perfect, the best he can remember. By now, in the first week of June, in all its green rows abundance is straining against order. There is not a weed in it. Though he has worked every day, he has had to measure the work out in little stints, and between stints he has had to rest.

But rest, this morning, has not come to him. When he went out after breakfast he saw Nathan turning the cows and calves into the Shade Field, so called for the woods that grows there on the slope above the stream called Shade Branch. He did not worry about it then, or while he worked through his morning jobs. But when he came out onto the porch and sat down and lit his pipe, a thought that had been on its way toward him for several hours finally reached him. He does not know how good the line fence is down Shade Branch; he would bet that Nathan, who is still rushing to get his crops out, has not looked at it. The panic of a realized neglect came upon him. It has been years since he has walked that fence himself, and he can see in his mind, as clearly as if he were there, perhaps five places where the winter spates of Shade Branch might have torn out the wire.

He sits, listening to Margaret, looking at pipe smoke, anxiously working his way down along that boundary in his mind.

"Mat," Margaret says at the screen door, "dinner's ready."

"All right," he says, though for perhaps a minute after that he does not move. And then he gets up, steps to the edge of the porch to knock out his pipe, and goes in.

When he has eaten, seeing him pick up his hat again from the chair by the door, Margaret says, "You're not going to take your nap?"

"No," he says, for he has decided to walk that length of the boundary line that runs down Shade Branch. And he has stepped beyond the feeling that he is going to do it because he should. He is going to do it because he wants to. "I got something yet I have to do."

He means to go on out the door without looking back. But he knows that she is watching him, worried about him, and he goes back to her and gives her a hug. "It's all right, my old girl," he says. He stands with his arms around her, who seems to him to have changed almost while he has held her from girl to wife to woman to mother to grandmother to great-grandmother. There in the old room where they have been together so long, ready again to leave it, he thinks, "I am an old man now."

"Don't worry," he says. "I'm feeling good."

He does feel good, for an old man, and once outside, he puts the house behind him and his journey ahead of him. At the barn he takes from its nail in the old harness room a stout stockman's cane. He does not need a cane yet, and he is proud of it, but as a concession to Margaret he has decided to carry one today.

When he lets himself out through the lot gate and into the open, past the barn and the other buildings, he can see the country lying under the sun. Nearby, on his own ridges, the crops are young and growing, the pastures are lush, a field of hay has been raked into curving windrows. Inlets of woods, in the perfect foliage of the early season, reach up the hollows between the ridges. Lower down, these various inlets join in the larger woods embayed in the little valley of Shade Branch. Beyond the ridges and hollows of the farm he can see the opening of the river valley, and beyond that the hills on the far side, blue in the distance.

He has it all before him, this place that has been his life, and how lightly and happily now he walks out again into it! It seems to him that he has cast off all restraint, left all encumbrances behind, taking only himself and his direction. He is feeling good. There has been plenty of rain, and the year is full of promise. The country looks promising. He thinks of the men he knows who are at work in it: the Coulter brothers and Nathan, Nathan's boy, Mattie, Elton Penn, and Mat's grandson, Bess's and Wheeler's boy, Andy Catlett. They are at Elton's now, he thinks, but by midafternoon they should be back here, baling the hay.

Carrying the cane over his shoulder, he crosses two fields, and then, letting himself through a third gate, turns right along the fencerow that will lead him down to Shade Branch. Soon he is walking steeply downward among the trunks of trees, and the shifting green sea of their foliage has closed over him.

He comes into the deeper shade of the older part of the woods where there is little browse and the cattle seldom come, and here he sits down at the root of an old white oak to rest. As many times before, he feels coming to him the freedom of the woods, where he has no work to do. He feels coming to him such rest as, bound to house and barn and garden for so long, he had forgot. In body, now, he is an old man, but mind and eye look out of his old body into the shifting leafy lights and shadows among the still trunks with a recognition that is without age, the return of an ageless joy. He needs the rest, for he has walked in his gladness at a faster pace than he is used to, and he is sweating. But he is in no hurry, and he sits and grows quiet among the sights and sounds of the place. The time of the most abundant blooming of the woods flowers is past now, but the tent villages of mayapple are still perfect, there are ferns and stonecrop, and near him he can see the candle-like white flowers of black cohosh. Below him, but still out of sight, he can hear the water in Shade Branch passing down over the rocks in a hundred little rapids and falls. When he feels the sweat beginning to dry on his face he gets up, braces himself against the gray trunk of the oak until he is steady, and stands free. The descent beckons and he yields eagerly to it, going on down into the tireless chanting of the stream.

He reaches the edge of the stream at a point where the boundary, coming down the slope facing him, turns at a right angle and follows Shade Branch in its fall toward the creek known as Willow Run. Here the fence that Mat has been following crosses the branch over the top of a rock wall that was built in the notch of the stream long before Mat was born. The water coming down, slowed by the wall, has filled the notch above it with rock and silt, and then, in freshet, leaping over it, has scooped out a shallow pool below it, where water stands most of the year. All this, given the continuous little changes of growth and wear in the woods and the stream, is as it was when Mat first knew it: the wall gray and mossy, the water, only a spout now, pouring over the wall into the little pool, covering the face of it with concentric wrinkles sliding outward.

Here, seventy-five years ago, Mat came with a fencing crew: his father, Ben, his uncle, Jack Beechum, Joe Banion, a boy then, not much older than Mat, and Joe's grandfather, Smoke, who had been a slave. And Mat remembers Jack Beechum coming down through the woods, as Mat himself has just come, carrying on his shoulder two of the long light rams they used to tamp the dirt into postholes.

As he approached the pool he took a ram in each hand, holding them high, made three long approaching strides, planted the rams in the middle of the pool, and vaulted over. Mat, delighted, said, "Do it again!" And without breaking rhythm, Jack turned, made the three swinging strides, and did it again—*does* it again in Mat's memory, so clearly that Mat's presence there, so long after, fades away, and he hears their old laughter, and hears Joe Banion say, "Mistah Jack, he might nigh a *bird*!"

Forty-some years later, coming down the same way to build that same fence again, Mat and Joe Banion and Virgil, Mat's son, grown then and full of the newness of his man's strength, Mat remembered what Jack had done and told Virgil; Virgil took the two rams, made the same three strides that Jack had made, vaulted the pool, and turned back and grinned. Mat and Joe Banion laughed again, and this time Joe looked at Mat and said only "Damn."

Now a voice in Mat's mind that he did not want to hear says, "Gone. All of them are gone." And they *are* gone. Mat is standing by the pool, and all the others are gone, and all that time has passed. And still the stream pours into the pool and the circles slide across its face.

He shrugs as a man would shake snow from his shoulders and steps away. He finds a good place to cross the branch, and picks his way carefully from rock to rock to the other side, using the cane for that and glad he brought it. Now he gives attention to the fence. Soon he comes upon signs—new wire spliced into the old, a staple newly driven into a sycamore—that tell him his fears were unfounded. Nathan has been here. For a while now Mat walks in the way he knows that Nathan went. Nathan is forty-one this year, a quiet, careful man, as attentive to Mat as Virgil might have been if Virgil had lived to return from the war. Usually, when Nathan has done such a piece of work as this, he will tell Mat so that Mat can have the satisfaction of knowing that the job is done. Sometimes, though, when he is hurried, he forgets, and Mat will think of the job and worry about it and finally go to see to it himself, almost always to find, as now, that Nathan has been there ahead of him and has done what needed to be done. Mat praises Nathan in his mind and calls him son. He has never called Nathan son aloud, to his face, for he does not wish to impose or intrude. But Nathan, who is not his son, has become his son, just as Hannah, Nathan's wife, Virgil's widow, who is not Mat's daughter, has become his daughter.

"I am blessed," he thinks. He walks in the way Nathan walked down along the fence, between the fence and the stream, seeing Nathan in his mind as clearly as if he were following close behind him, watching. He can see Nathan with axe and hammer and pliers and pail of staples and wire stretcher and coil of wire, making his way down along the fence, stopping now to chop a windfall off the wire and retighten it, stopping again to staple the fence to a young sycamore that has grown up in the line opportunely to serve as a post. Mat can imagine every move Nathan made, and in his old body, a little tired now, needing to be coaxed and instructed in the passing of obstacles, he remembers the strength of the body of a man of forty-one, unregarding of its own effort.

Now, trusting the fence to Nathan, Mat's mind turns away from it. He allows himself to drift down the course of the stream, passing through it as the water passes, drawn by gravity, bemused by its little chutes and falls. He stops beside one tiny quiet backwater and watches a family of water striders conducting their daily business, their feet dimpling the surface. He eases the end of his cane into the pool, and makes a crawfish spurt suddenly backward beneath a rock.

A water thrush moves down along the rocks of the streambed

ahead of him, teetering and singing. He stops and stands to watch while a large striped woodpecker works its way up the trunk of a big sycamore, putting its eye close to peer under the loose scales of the bark. And then the bird flies to its nesting hole in a hollow snag still nearer by to feed its young, paying Mat no mind. He has become still as a tree, and now a hawk suddenly stands on a limb close over his head. The hawk loosens his feathers and shrugs, looking around him with his fierce eyes. And it comes to Mat that once more, by stillness, he has passed across into the wild inward presence of the place.

"Wonders," he thinks. "Little wonders of a great wonder." He feels the sweetness of time. If a man eighty years old has not seen enough, then nobody will ever see enough. Such a little piece of the world as he has before him now would be worth a man's long life, watching and listening. And then he could go two hundred feet and live again another life, listening and watching, and his eyes would never be satisfied with seeing, nor his ears filled with hearing. Whatever he saw could be seen only by looking away from something else equally worth seeing. For a second he feels and then loses some urging of the delight in a mind that could see and comprehend it all, all at once. "I could stay here a long time," he thinks. "I could stay here a long time."

He is standing at the head of a larger pool, another made by the plunging of the water over a rock wall. This one he built himself, he and Virgil, in the terribly dry summer of 1930. By the latter part of that summer, because of the shortage of both rain and money, they had little enough to do, and they had water on their minds. Mat remembered this place, where a strong vein of water opened under the roots of a huge old sycamore and flowed only a few feet before it sank uselessly among the dry stones of the streambed. "We'll make a pool," he said. He and Virgil worked several days in the August of that year, building the wall and filling in behind it so that the stream, when it ran full again, would not tear out the stones. The work there in the depth of the woods took their minds off their parched fields and comforted them. It was a kind of work that Mat loved and taught Virgil to love, requiring only the simplest tools: a large sledgehammer, a small one, and two heavy crowbars with which they moved the big, thick rocks that were in that place. Once their tools were there, they left them until the job was done. When they came down to work they brought only a jug of water from the cistern at the barn.

"We could drink out of the spring," Virgil said.

"Of course we could," Mat said. "It's dog days now. Do you want to get sick?"

In a shady place near the creek, Virgil tilted a flagstone up against a small sycamore, wedging it between trunk and root, to make a place for the water jug. There was not much reason for that. It was a thing a boy would do, making a little domestic nook like that, so far off in the woods, but Mat shared his pleasure in it, and that was where they kept the jug.

When they finished the work and carried their tools away, they left the jug, forgot it, and did not go back to get it. Mat did not think of it again until, years later, he happened to notice the rock still leaning against the tree, which had grown over it, top and bottom, fastening the rock to itself by a kind of natural mortise. Looking under the rock, Mat found the earthen jug still there, though it had been broken by the force of the tree trunk growing against it. He left it as it was. By then Virgil was dead, and the stream, rushing over the wall they had made, had scooped out a sizable pool that had been a faithful water source in dry years.

Remembering, Mat goes to the place and looks and again finds the stone and finds the broken jug beneath it. He has never touched rock or jug, and he does not do so now. He stands, looking, thinking of his son, dead twenty years, a stranger to his daughter, now a grown woman, who never saw him, and he says aloud, "Poor fellow!" So taken is his mind by his thoughts that he does not know he is weeping until he feels his tears cool on his face.

Deliberately, he turns away. Deliberately, he gives his mind back to the day and the stream. He goes on down beside the flowing water, loitering, listening to the changes in its voice as he walks along it. He silences his mind now and lets the stream speak for him, going on, descending with it, only to prolong his deep peaceable attention to that voice that speaks always only of where it is, remembering nothing, fearing and desiring nothing.

Farther down, the woods thinning somewhat, he can see ahead of him where the Shade Branch hollow opens into the valley of Willow Run. He can see the crest of the wooded slope on the far side of the creek valley. He stops. For a minute or so his mind continues on beyond him, charmed by the juncture he has come to. He imagines the succession of them, openings on openings: Willow Run opening to the Kentucky River, the Kentucky to the Ohio, the Ohio to the Mississippi, the Mississippi to the Gulf of Mexico, the Gulf to the boundless sky. He walks in old memory out into the river, carrying a heavy rock in each hand, out and down, until the water closes over his head and then the light shudders above him and disappears, and he walks in the dark cold water, down the slant of the bottom, to the limit of breath, and then drops his weights and cleaves upward into light and air again.

He turns around and faces the way he has come. "*Well*, old man!" he thinks. "*Now* what are you going to do?" For he has come down a long way, and now, looking back, he feels the whole country tilted against him. He feels the weight of it and the hot light over it. He hears himself say aloud, "Why, I've got to get back out of here."

But he is tired. It has been a year since he has walked even so far as he has already come. He feels the heaviness of his body, a burden that, his hand tells him, he has begun to try to shift off his legs and onto the cane. He thinks of Margaret, who, he knows as well as he knows anything, already wonders where he is and is worrying about him. Fear and exasperation hold him for a moment, but he pushes them off; he forces himself to be patient with himself. "Well," he says, as if joking with Virgil, for Virgil has come back into his thoughts now as a small boy, "going up ain't the same as coming down. It's going to be different."

It would be possible to go on down, and he considers that. He could follow the branch on down to the Willow Run road where it passes the Rowanberry place. That would be downhill, and if he could find Mart Rowanberry near the house, Mart would give him a ride home. But the creek road is little traveled these days; if he goes down there and Mart is up on the ridge at work, which he probably is, then Mat will be farther from home than he is now, and will have a long walk, at least as far as the blacktop, maybe farther. Of course, he could go down there and just wait until Mart comes to the house at quitting time. There is sense in that, and for a moment Mat stands balanced between ways. What finally decides him is that he is unsure what lies between him and the creek road. If he goes down much farther he will cross the line fence onto the Rowanberry place. He knows that he would be all right for a while, going on down along the branch, but once in the creek bottom he would have to make his way to the road through dense, undergrowthy thicket, made worse maybe by piles of drift left by the winter's high water.

He might have trouble getting through there, he thinks, and the strangeness of that place seems to forbid him. It has begun to trouble him that no other soul on earth knows where he is. He does not want to go where he will not know where he is himself.

He chooses the difficult familiar way, and steps back into it, helping himself with the cane now. He does immediately feel the difference between coming down and going up, and he wanders this way and that across the line of his direction, searching for the easiest steps. Windfalls that he went around or stepped over thoughtlessly, coming down, now require him to stop and study and choose. He is tired. He moves by choice.

He and his father have come down the branch, looking for a heifer due to calve; they have found her and are going back. Mat is tired. He wants to be home, but he does not want to *go* home. He is hot and a scratch on his face stings with sweat. He would just as soon cry as not, and his father, walking way up ahead of him, has not even slowed down. Mat cries, "*Wait*, Papa!" And his father does turn and wait, a man taller than he looks because of the breadth of his shoulders, whom Mat would never see in a hurry and rarely see at rest. He has turned, smiling in the heavy bush of his beard, looking much as he will always look in Mat's memory of him, for Mat was born too late to know him young and he would be dead before he was old. "Come on, Mat," Ben says. "Come on, my boy." As Mat comes up to him, he reaches down with a big hand that Mat puts his hand into. "It's all right. It ain't that far." They go on up the branch then. When they come to a windfall across the branch, Ben says, "This one we go under." And when they come to another, he says, "This one we go around."

Mat, who came down late in the afternoon to fix the fence, has fixed it, and is hurrying back, past chore time, and he can hear Virgil behind him, calling to him, "Wait, Daddy!" He brought Virgil against his better judgment, because Virgil would not be persuaded not to come. "You need me," he said. "I do need you," Mat said, won over. "You're my right-hand man. Come on." But now, irritated with himself and with Virgil too, he knows that Virgil needs to be carried, but his hands are loaded with tools and he *can't* carry him. Or so he tells himself, and he walks on. He stretches the distance out between them until Virgil feels that he has been left alone in the darkening woods; he sits down on a rock and gives himself up to grief. Hearing him cry, Mat puts his tools down where he can find them in the morning, and goes back for Virgil. "Well, it's all right, old boy," he says, picking him up. "It's all right. It's all right."

He is all right, but he is sitting down on a tree trunk lying across the branch, and he has not been able to persuade himself to get up. He came up to the fallen tree, and, to his surprise, instead of stepping over it, he sat down on it. At first that seemed to him the proper thing to do. He needed to sit down. He was tired. But now a protest begins in his mind. He needs to be on his way. He ought to be home by now. He knows that Margaret has been listening for him. He knows that several times by now she has paused in her work and listened, and gone to the windows to look out. She is hulling the peas he brought her before dinner. If he were there, he would be helping her. He thinks of the two of them sitting in the kitchen, hulling peas, and talking. Such a sense of luxury has come into their talk, now that they are old and in no hurry. They talk of what they know in common and do not need to talk about, and so talk about only for pleasure.

They would talk about where everybody is today and what each one is doing. They would talk about the stock and the crops. They would talk about how nice the peas are this year, and how good the garden is.

He thought, once, that maybe they would not have a garden. There were reasons not to have one.

"We don't need a garden this year," he said to Margaret, wanting to spare her the work that would be in it for her.

"Yes," she said, wanting to spare him the loss of the garden, "of course we do!"

"Margaret, we'll go to all that work, and can all that food, and neither one of us may live to eat it."

She gave him her smile, then, the same smile she had always given him, that always seemed to him to have survived already the worst he could think of. She said, "Somebody will."

She pleased him, and the garden pleased him. After even so many years, he still needed to be bringing something to her.

His command to get up seems to prop itself against his body and stay there like a brace until finally, in its own good time and again to his surprise, his body obeys. He gets up, steps over the tree, and goes on. He keeps himself on his feet for some time now, herding himself along like a recalcitrant animal, searching for the easy steps, reconciling himself to the hard steps when there are no easy ones. He is sweating heavily. The air is hot and close, so deep in that cleft of the hill. He feels that he must stretch upward to breathe. It is as though his body has come to belong in a different element, and the mere air of that place now hardly sustains it.

He comes to the pool, the wall that he and Virgil made, and pauses there. "Now you must drink," he says. He goes to where the spring comes up among the roots of the sycamore. There is a smooth clear pool there, no bigger than his hat. He lies down to drink, and drinks, looking down into the tiny pool cupped among the roots, surrounded with stonecrop and moss. The loveliness of it holds him: the cool water in that pretty place in the shade, the great tree rising and spreading its white limbs overhead. "I am blessed," he thinks, "I could stay here." He rests where he lies, turned away from his drinking, more comfortable on the roots and rocks than he expected to be. Through the foliage he can see white clouds moving along as if mindful where they are going. A chipmunk comes in quick starts and stops across the rocks and crouches a long time not far from Mat's face, watching him, as if perhaps it would like a drink from the little pool that Mat just drank from. "Come on," Mat says to it. "There ain't any harm in me." He would like to sleep. There is a weariness beyond weariness in him that sleep would answer. He can remember a time when he could have let himself sleep in such a place, but he cannot do that now. "Get up," he says aloud. "Get up, get up."

But for a while yet he does not move. He and the chipmunk watch each other. Now and again their minds seem to wander apart, and then they look again and find each other still there. There is a sound of wings, like a sudden dash of rain, and the chipmunk tumbles off its rock and does not appear again. Mat laughs. "You'd *better* hide." And now he does get up.

He stands, his left hand propped against the trunk of the syca-more. Darkness draws across his vision and he sinks back down onto his knees, his right hand finding purchase in the cold cup of the spring. The darkness wraps closely around him for a time, and then withdraws, and he stands again. "*That* won't do," he says to Virgil. "We got to do better than that, boy." And then he sees his father too standing with Virgil on the other side of the stream. They recognize him, even though he is so much older now than when they knew him—older than either of them ever lived to be. "Well," he says, "looks like we got plenty of help." He reaches down and lets his right hand feel its way to the cane, picks it up, and straightens again. "*Yes*sir."

The world clears, steadies, and levels itself again in the light. He looks around him at the place: the wall, the pool, the spring mossy and clear in the roots of the white tree. "I am not going to come back here," he thinks. "I will never be in this place again."

Instructing his steps, he leaves. He moves with the utmost care and the utmost patience. For some time he does not think of where he is going. He is merely going up along the stream, asking first for one step and then for the next, moving by little plans that he carefully makes, and by choice. When he pauses to catch his breath or consider his way, he can feel his heart beating; at each of its beats the world seems to dilate and spring away from him.

His father and Virgil are with him, moving along up the opposite side of the branch as he moves up his side. He cannot always see them, but he knows they are there. First he does not see them, and then he sees one or the other of them appear among the trees and stand looking at him. They do not speak, though now and again he speaks to them. And then Jack Beechum, Joe Banion, and old Smoke are with them. He sees them sometimes separately, sometimes together. The dead who were here with him before are here with him again. He is not afraid. "I could stay here," he thinks. But ahead of him there is a reason he should not do that, and he goes on.

He seems to be walking in and out of his mind. Or it is time, perhaps, that he is walking in and out of. Sometimes he is with the dead as they were, and he is as he was, and all of them together are walking upward through the woods toward home. Sometimes he is alone, an old man in a later time than any of the dead have known, going the one way that he alone is going, among all the ways he has gone before, among all the ways he has never gone and will never go.

He does not remember falling. He is lying on the rocks beside the branch, and there is such disorder and discomfort in the way he is lying as he could not have intended. And so he must have fallen. He wonders if he is going to get up. After a while he does at least sit up. He shifts around so that his back can rest against the trunk of a tree. His movements cause little lurches in the world, and he waits for it to be steady. "Now you have got to stop and think," he says. And then he says, "Well, you have stopped. Now you had better think."

He does begin to think, forcing his vision and his thoughts out away from him into the place around him, his mind making little articulations of recognition. The place and his memory of it begin to speak to one another. He has come back almost to the upper wall and pool, where he first came down to the branch. When he gets there he will have a choice to make between two hard ways to go.

But his mind, having thought of those choices, now leaves him, like an undisciplined pup, and goes to the house, and goes back in time to the house the way it was when he and Margaret were still young, when Virgil was four or five years old, and Bess was eleven or twelve.

About this time in the afternoon, about this time in the year, having come to the house for something, he cannot remember what, he pushes open the kitchen door, leans his shoulder on the jamb, and looks at Margaret who stands with her back to him, icing a cake.

"Now nobody's asked for my opinion," he says, "and nobody's likely to, but if anybody ever was to, I'd say that *that* is a huggable woman."

"Don't you come near me, Mat Feltner."

"And a spirited woman."

"If you so much as lay a hand on me, I'm going to hit you with this cake."

"And a dangerous, mean woman."

"Go back to work."

"Who is, still and all, a huggable woman. Which is only my opinion. A smarter man might think different."

She turns around, laughing, and comes to get her hug. "I could never have married a smart man."

"She didn't marry *too* smart a one," he thinks. He is getting up, the effort requiring the attendance of his mind, and once he is standing he puts his mind back on his problem. That is not where it wants to be, but this time he makes it stay. If he leaves the branch and goes back up onto the ridge by the way he came down, that will require a long slanting climb up across the face of a steep slope. "And it has got steeper since I came down it," he thinks. If he goes on up Shade Branch, which would be the easiest, surest route, he will have, somehow, to get over or through the fence that crosses the branch above the wall. He does not believe that he can climb the fence. Where the fence crosses the stream it is of barbed wire, and in that place a stronger man might go through or under it. But he does not want to risk hooking his clothes on the barbs.

But now he thinks of a third possibility: the ravine that comes into Shade Branch just above him to his right hand. The dry, rocky streambed in the ravine would go up more gently than the slope, the rocks would afford him stairsteps of a sort for at least some of the way, and it would be the shortest way out of the woods. It would bring him out farther from home than the other ways, but he must not let that bother him. It is the most possible of the three ways, and the most important thing now, he knows, is to get up onto the open land of the ridge where he can be seen if somebody comes looking for him. Somebody will be looking for him, he hopes, for he has to admit that he is not going very fast, and once he starts up the ravine he will be going slower than ever.

For a while he kept up the belief, and then the hope, that he could make it home in a reasonable time and walk into the house as if nothing had happened.

"Where on earth have you been?" Margaret would ask.

He would go to the sink to wash up, and then he would say, drying his hands, "Oh, I went to see about the line fence down the branch, but Nathan had already fixed it."

He would sit down then to help her with the peas.

"Mat Feltner," she would say, "surely you didn't go away off down there."

But it is too late now, for something *has* happened. He has been gone too long, and is going to be gone longer.

Margaret has got up from her work and gone to the windows and looked out, and gone to the door onto the back porch and spoken his name, and walked on out to the garden gate and then to the gate to the barn lot.

He can see her and hear her calling as plainly as if he were haunting her. "Mat! Oh, Mat!"

He can hear her, and he makes his way on up the branch to the mouth of the ravine. He turns up the bed of the smaller stream. The climb is steeper here, the hard steps closer together. The ascent asks him now really to climb, and in places, where the rocks of the streambed bulge outward in a wall, he must help himself with his hands. He must stoop under and climb over the trunks of fallen trees. When he stops after each of these efforts the heavy beating of his heart keeps on. He can feel it shaking him, and darkness throbs in his eyes. His breaths come too far between and too small. Sometimes he has roots along the side of the ravine for a banister, and that helps. Sometimes the cane helps; sometimes, when he needs both hands, it is in the way. And always he is in the company of the dead.

Ahead of him the way is closed by the branchy top of a young maple, blown down in a storm, and he must climb up the side of the ravine to get around it. At the top of the climb, when the slope has gentled and he stops and his heart plunges on and his vision darkens, it seems to him that he is going to fall; he decides instead to sit down, and does. Slowly he steadies again within himself. His heart slows and his vision brightens again. He tells himself again to get up. "It ain't as far as it has been," he says to Virgil. "I'm going to be all right now. I'm going to make it."

But now his will presses against his body, as if caught within it, in bewilderment. It will not move. There was a time when his body had strength enough in it to carry him running up such a place as this, with breath left over to shout. There was a time when it had barely enough strength in it to carry it this far. There is a time when his body is too heavy for his strength. He longs to lie down. To Jack Beechum, the young man, Jack Beechum, who is watching him now, he says, "You and I were here once."

The dead come near him, and he is among them. They come and go, appear and disappear, like a flock of feeding birds. They are there and gone. He is among them, and then he is alone. To one who is not going any farther, it is a pretty place, the leaves new and perfect, a bird singing out of sight among them somewhere over his head, and the softening light slanting in long beams from the west. "I could stay here," he thinks. It is the thought of going on that turns that steep place into an agony. His own stillness pacifies it and makes it lovely. He thinks of dying, secretly, by himself, in the woods. No one now knows where he is. Perhaps it would be possible to hide and die, and never be found. It would be a clean, clear way for that business to be done, and the thought, in his weariness, comforts him, for he has feared that he might die a nuisance to Margaret and the others. He might, perhaps, hide himself in a little cave or sink hole if one were nearby, here where the dead already are, and be one of them, and enter directly into the peaceableness of this place, and turn with it through the seasons, his body grown easy in its weight.

But there is no hiding place. He would be missed and hunted for and found. He would die a nuisance, for he could not hide from all the reasons that he would be missed and worried about and hunted for. He has an appointment that must be kept, and between him and it the climb rises on above him.

He has an accounting he must come to, and it is not with the dead, for Margaret has not sat down again, but is walking. She is walking from room to room and from window to window. She has not called Bess, because she does not want Bess to drive all the way up from Hargrave, perhaps for nothing. Though she has thought about it, she has not even called Hannah, who is nearer by. She does not want to alarm anybody. But she is alarmed. She walks from room to room and from window to window, pausing to look out, and walking again. She walks with her arms tightly folded, as she has walked all her life when she has been troubled, until Mat, watching her, has imagined that he thinks as she thinks and feels as she feels, so moved by her at times that he has been startled to realize again his separateness from her.

He remembers the smile of assent that she gave him once: "Why, Mat, I thought you did. And I love you." Everything that has happened to him since has come from that—and leads to that, for it is not a moment that has ever stopped happening; he has gone toward it and aspired to it all his life, a time that he has not surpassed.

Now she is an old woman, walking in his mind in the rooms of their house. She has called no one and told no one. She is the only one who knows that she does not know where he is. The men are in the hayfield, and she is waiting for one of them or some of them to come to the barn. Or Wheeler might come by. It is the time of day when he sometimes does. She walks slowly from room to room, her arms folded tightly, and she watches the windows.

Mat, sitting in his heaviness among the trees, she does not know where, yearns for her as from beyond the grave. "Don't worry," he says. "It's going to be all right." He gets up.

And now an overmastering prayer that he did not think to pray rushes upon him out of the air and seizes him and grapples him to itself: an absolute offering of himself to his return. It is an offer, involuntary as his breath, voluntary as the new steps he has already taken up the hill, to give up his life in order to have it. The prayer does not move him beyond weariness and weakness, it moves him merely beyond all other thoughts.

He gives no more regard to death or to the dead. The dead do not appear again. Now he is walking in this world, walking in time, going home. A shadowless love moves him now, not his, but a love that he belongs to, as he belongs to the place and to the light over it. He is thinking of Margaret and of all that his plighting with her has led to. He is thinking of the membership of the fields that he has belonged to all his life, and will belong to while he breathes, and afterward. He is thinking of the living ones of that membership—at work today in the fields that the dead were at work in before them.

"I am blessed," he thinks. "I am blessed."

He is crawling now, the cane lost and forgotten. He crawls a little, and he rests a lot. The slope has gentled somewhat. The big woods has given way to thicket. He has turned away from the stream, taking the straightest way to the open slope that he can see not far above him. The cattle are up there grazing, the calves starting to play a little, now that the cool of the day is here.

When he comes out, clear of the trees, onto the grassed hillside, he seems again to have used up all his strength. "Now," he thinks, "you have got to rest." Once he has rested he will go on to the top of the ridge. Once he gets there, he can make it to the road. He crawls on up the slope a few feet to where a large walnut tree stands alone outside the woods, and sits against it so that he will have a prop for his back. He wipes his face, brushes at the dirt and litter on his knees and then subsides. Not meaning to, he sleeps.

The sun is going down when he wakes, the air cold on his damp clothes. Except for opening his eyes, he does not move. His body is still as a stone.

Now he knows what woke him. It is the murmur of an automobile engine up on the ridge—Wheeler's automobile, by the sound of it. And when it comes into sight he sees that it is Wheeler's; Wheeler is driving and Elton Penn and Nathan are with him. They are not looking for him. They have not seen Margaret. Perhaps they did not bale the hay. Or they may have finished and got away early. But he knows that Wheeler found Nathan and Elton, wherever they were, after he shut his office and drove up from Hargrave, and they have been driving from field to field ever since, at Elton's place or at Nathan's or at Wheeler's, and now here. This is something they do, Mat knows, for he is often with them when they do it. Wheeler drives the car slowly, and they look and worry and admire and remember and plan. They have come to look at the cattle now, to see them on the new grass. They move among the cows and calves, looking and stopping. Now and then an arm reaches out of one of the car windows and points. For a long time they do not turn toward Mat. It is as though he is only part of the field, like the tree he is leaning against. He feels the strangeness of his stillness, but he does not move.

And then, still a considerable distance away, Wheeler turns the car straight toward the tree where Mat is sitting. He sees their heads go up when they see him, and he raises his right hand and gives them what, for all his eagerness, is only an ordinary little wave.

Wheeler accelerates, and the car comes tilting and rocking down the slope. Where the slope steepens, forcing the car to slow down, Mat sees Nathan leap out of it and come running toward him, Elton out too, then, coming behind him, while Wheeler is still maneuvering the car down the hill. Seeing that they are running to help him, Mat despises his stillness. He forces himself to his knees and then to his feet. He turns to face Nathan, who has almost reached him. He lets go of the tree and stands, and sees the ground rising against him like a blow. He feels himself caught strongly, steadied, and held. He hears himself say, "Papa?"

That night, when Margaret finds him wandering in the darkened house, he does not know where he is.

That Distant Land

(*1965*)

For several days after the onset of his decline, my grandfather's mind seemed to leave him to go wandering, lost, in some foreign place. It was a dream he was in, we thought, that he could not escape. He was looking for the way home, and he could not find anyone who knew how to get there.

"No," he would say. "Port William. Port William is the name of the place."

Or he would ask, "Would you happen to know a nice lady by the name of Margaret Feltner? She lives in Port William. Now, which way would I take to get there?"

But it was not us he was asking. He was not looking at us and mistaking us for other people. He was not looking at us at all. He was talking to people he was meeting in his dream. From the way he spoke to them, they seemed to be nice people. They treated him politely and were kind, but they did not know any of the things that he knew, and they could not help him.

When his mind returned, it did so quietly. It had never been a mind that made a lot of commotion around itself. One morning when my grandmother went in to wake him and he opened his eyes, they were looking again. He looked at my grandmother and said, "Margaret, I'll declare." He looked around him at the bright room and out the window at the ridges and the woods, and said, "You got a nice place here, ma'am."

My grandmother, as joyful as if he had indeed been gone far away and had come home, said, "Oh, Mat, are you all right?"

And he said, "I seem to be a man who has been all right before, and I'm all right now."

That was the middle of June, and having come back from wherever it had been, his mind stayed with him and with us, a peaceable, pleasant guest, until he died.

He did not get out of bed again. What troubled us, and then grieved us, and finally consoled us, was that he made no effort to get up. It appeared to us that he felt his time of struggle to be past, and that he agreed to its end. He who had lived by ceaseless effort now lived simply as his life was given to him, day by day. During the time his mind had wandered he ate little or nothing, and though his mind returned his appetite did not. He ate to please my grandmother, but he could not eat much. She would offer the food, he would eat the few bites that were enough, and she would take the plate away. None of us had the heart to go beyond her gentle offering. No one insisted. No one begged. He asked almost nothing of us, only to be there with us, and we asked only to be with him.

He lay in a room on the east side of the house, so that from the window he could look out across the ridges toward the river valley. And he did often lie there looking out. Now that he felt his own claims removed from it, the place seemed to have become more than ever interesting to him, and he watched it as the dark lifted from it and the sun rose and moved above it and set and the dark returned. Now and then he would speak of what he saw—the valley brimming with fog in the early morning, a hawk circling high over the ridges, somebody at work in one of the fields—and we would know that he watched with understanding and affection. But the character of his watching had changed. We all felt it. We had known him as a man who watched, but then his watching had been purposeful. He had watched as a man preparing for what he knew he must do, and what he wanted to do. Now it had become the watching, almost, of one who was absent.

The room was bright in the mornings, and in the afternoons dim and cool. It was always clean and orderly. My grandfather, who had no wants, made no clutter around him, and any clutter that the rest of us made did not last long. His room became the center of the house, where we came to rest. He would welcome us, raising his hand to us as we came in, listening to all that was said, now and again saying something himself.

Because, wherever we were, we kept him in our minds, he kept us together in the world as we knew he kept us in his mind. Until the night of his death we were never all in the house at the same time, yet no day passed that he did not see most of us. In the morning, my mother, his only surviving child, or Hannah Coulter, who had been his daughter-in-law and was, in all but blood, his daughter, or Flora, my wife, or Sara, my brother Henry's wife, would come in to spend the day with my grandmother to keep her company and help with the work. And at evening my father, or Henry, or I, or Nathan

Coulter, who now farmed my grandfather's farm and was, in all but blood, his son, would come, turn about, to spend the night, to give whatever help would be needed.

And others who were not family came: Burley Coulter, Burley's brother Jarrat, Elton and Mary Penn, Arthur and Martin Rowanberry. They would happen by for a few minutes in the daytime, or come after supper and sit and talk an hour or two. We were a membership. We belonged together, and my grandfather's illness made us feel it.

But "illness," now that I have said it, seems the wrong word. It was not like other illnesses that I had seen—it was quieter and more peaceable. It was, it would be truer to say, a great weariness that had come upon him, like the lesser weariness that comes with the day's end—a weariness that had been earned, and was therefore accepted.

I had lived away, working in the city, for several years, and had returned home only that spring. I was thirty-one years old, I had a wife and children, and my return had given a sudden sharp clarity to my understanding of my home country. Every fold of the land, every grass blade and leaf of it gave me joy, for I saw how my own place in it had been prepared, along with its failures and its losses. Though I knew that I had returned to difficulties—not the least of which were the deaths that I could see coming—I was joyful.

The nights I spent, taking my turn, on the cot in a corner of my grandfather's room gave me a strong, sweet pleasure. At first, usually, visitors would be there, neighbors or family stopping by. Toward bedtime, they would go. I would sit on a while with my grandmother and grandfather, and we would talk. Or rather, if I could arrange it so, they would talk and I would listen. I loved to start them talking about old times—my mother's girlhood, their own young years, stories told them by their parents and grandparents, memories of memories. In their talk the history of Port William went back and back along one of its lineages until it ended in silence and conjecture, for Port William was older than its memories. That it had begun we knew because it had continued, but we did not know when or how it had begun.

It was usually easy enough to get them started, for they enjoyed the remembering, and they knew that I liked to hear. "Grandad," I would say, "who was George Washington Coulter's mother?" Or: "Granny, tell about Aunt Maude Wheeler hailing the steamboat." And they would enter the endlessly varying pattern of remembering. A name would remind them of a story; one story would remind them of another. Sometimes my grandmother would get out a box of old photographs and we would sit close to the bed so that my grandfather could see them too, and then the memories and names moved and hovered over the transfixed old sights. The picture that most moved and troubled me was the only consciously photographed "scene": a look down the one street of Port William at the time of my grandparents' childhood—1890 or thereabouts. What so impressed me about it was that the town had then been both more prosperous and more the center of its own attention than I had ever known it to be. The business buildings all had upper stories, the church had a steeple, there was a row of trees, planted at regular intervals, along either side of the road. Now the steeple and most of the upper stories were gone—by wind or fire or decay— and many of the trees were gone. For a long time, in Port William, what had gone had not been replaced. Its own attention had turned away from itself toward what it could not be. And I understood how, in his dream, my grandfather had suffered his absence from the town; through much of his life it had grown increasingly absent from itself.

After a while, my grandmother would leave us. She would go to my grandfather's side and take his hand. "Mat, is there anything you want before I go?"

"Ma'am," he would say, "I've got everything I want." He would be teasing her a little, as he was always apt to do.

She would hesitate, wishing, I think, that he did want something. "Well, good night. I'll see you in the morning."

And he would pat her hand and say very agreeably, as if he were altogether willing for that to happen, if it should happen, "All right."

She would go and we would hear her stirring about in her room, preparing for bed. I would do everything necessary to make my grandfather comfortable for the night, help him to relieve himself, help him to turn onto his side, straighten the bedclothes, see that the flashlight was in reach in case he wanted to look at the clock, which he sometimes did. I was moved by his willingness to let me help him. We had always been collaborators. When I was little, he had been the one in the family who would help me with whatever I was trying to make. And now he accepted help as cheerfully as he had given it. We were partners yet.

I was still a young man, with a young man's prejudice in favor of young bodies. I would have been sorry but I would not have been surprised if I had found it unpleasant to have to handle him as I did—his old flesh slackened and dwindling on the bones—but I did not find it so. I touched him gratefully. I would put one knee on the bed and gather him in my arms and move him toward me and turn him. I liked to do it. The comfort I gave him I felt. He would say, "Thanks, son."

When he was settled, I would turn on the dim little bedlamp by the cot and go to bed myself.

"Sleep tight," I would tell him.

"Well," he would say, amused, "I will part of the time."

I would read a while, letting the remembered dear stillness of the old house come around me, and then I would sleep.

My grandfather did only sleep part of the time. Mostly, when he was awake, he lay quietly with his thoughts, but sometimes he would have to call me, and I would get up to bring him a drink (he would want only two or three swallows), or help him to use the bedpan, or help him to turn over.

Once he woke me to recite me the Twenty-third Psalm. "Andy," he said. "Andy. Listen." He said the psalm to me. I lay listening to his old, slow voice coming through the dark to me, saying that he walked through the valley of the shadow of death and was not afraid. It stood my hair up. I had known that psalm all my life. I had heard it and said it a thousand times. But until then I had always felt that it came from a long way off, some place I had not lived. Now, hearing him speak it, it seemed to me for the first time to utter itself in our tongue and to wear our dust. My grandfather slept again after that, but I did not.

Another night, again, I heard him call me. "Andy. Listen." His voice exultant then, at having recovered the words, he recited:

> There entertain him all the saints above,
> In solemn troops and sweet societies
> That sing, and singing in their glory move,
> And wipe the tears forever from his eyes.

After he spoke them, the words stood above us in the dark and the quiet, sounding and luminous. And then they faded.

After a while I said, "Who taught you that?"

"My mother. She was a great hand to improve your mind."

And after a while, again, I asked, "Do you know who wrote it?"

"No," he said. "But wasn't he a fine one!"

As the summer went along, he weakened, but so slowly we could hardly see it happening. There was never any sudden change. He remained quiet, mainly comfortable, and alert. We stayed in our routine of caring for him; it had become the ordinary way of things.

In the latter part of August we started into the tobacco cutting. For us, that is the great divider of the year. It ends the summer, and makes safe the season's growth. After it, our minds are lightened, and we look ahead to winter and the coming year. It is a sort of ritual of remembrance, too, when we speak of other years and remember our younger selves and the absent and the dead—all those we have, as we say, "gone down the row with."

We had a big crew that year—eight men working every day: Jarrat and Burley and Nathan Coulter, Arthur and Martin Rowanberry, Elton Penn, Danny Branch, and me. Hannah Coulter and Mary Penn and Lyda Branch kept us fed and helped with the hauling and housing. And Nathan's and Hannah's boy, Mattie, and the Penns' children, Elsie and Jack, were with us until school started, and then they worked after school and on Saturdays. We worked back and forth among the various farms as the successive plantings became ready for harvest.

"What every tobacco cutting needs," Art Rowanberry said, "is a bunch of eighteen-year-old boys wanting to show how fast they are."

He was right, but we did not have them. We were not living in a time that was going to furnish many such boys for such work. Except for Mattie and Jack, who were fourteen and eleven, and would have liked to show how fast they were, if they had been fast, we were all old enough to be resigned to the speed we could stand. And so, when we cut, we would be strung out along the field in a pattern that never varied from the first day to the last. First would be Elton and Nathan and Danny, all working along together. Elton, I think, would have proved the fastest if anybody had challenged him, but nobody did. Then came Mart Rowanberry, who was always ahead of me, though he was nearly twice my age, and then, some distance behind me, would come Art Rowanberry, and then Burley Coulter, and then, far back, Burley's brother Jarrat, whose judgment and justification of himself were unswerving: "I'm old and wore out and not worth a damn. But every row I cut is a cut row."

In my grandfather's absence Jarrat was the oldest of us, a long-enduring, solitary, mostly silent man, slowed by age and much hard work. His brushy eyes could stare upon you as if you had no more ability to stare back than a post. When he had something to say, his way was simply to begin to say it, no matter who else was talking or what else was happening, his slow, hard-edged voice boring in upon us like his stare—and the result, invariably, was that whatever was happening stopped, and whoever was talking listened.

I never caught up with Elton and Nathan and Danny, or came anywhere near it, but at least when the rows were straight I always had them in sight, and I loved to watch them. Though they kept an even, steady pace, it was not a slow one. They drove into the work, maintaining the same pressing rhythm from one end of the row to the other, and yet they worked well, as smoothly and precisely as dancers. To see them moving side by side against the standing crop, leaving it fallen, the field changed, behind them, was maybe like watching Homeric soldiers going into battle. It was momentous and beautiful, and touchingly, touchingly mortal. They were spending themselves as they worked, giving up their time; they would not return by the way they went.

The good crew men among us were Burley and Elton. When the sun was hot and the going hard, it would put heart into us to hear Burley singing out down the row some scrap of human sorrow that his flat, exuberant voice both expressed and mocked:

Allll our sins and griefs to *bear*-oh!

—that much only, raised abruptly out of the silence like the howl of some solitary dog. Or he would sing with a lovelorn quaver in his voice:

Darlin', fool yourself and love me one more time.

And when we were unloading the wagons in the barn, he would start his interminable tale about his life as a circus teamster. It was not meant to be believed, and yet in our misery we listened to his extravagant wonderful lies as if he had been Marco Polo returned from Cathay.

Elton had as much gab as Burley, when he wanted to, but he served us as the teller of the tale of our own work. He told and retold everything that happened that was funny. That we already knew what he was telling, that he was telling us what we ourselves had done, did not matter. He told it well, he told it the way we would tell it when we told it, and every time he told it he told it better. He told us, also, how much of our work we had got done, and how much we had left to do, and how we might form the tasks still ahead in order to do them. His head, of course, was not the only one involved, and not the only good one, but his was indeed a good one, and his use of it pleased him and comforted us. Though we had a lot of work still to do, we were going to be able to do it, and these were the ways we could get it done. The whole of it stayed in his mind. He shaped it for us and gave it a comeliness greater than its difficulty.

That we were together now kept us reminded of my grandfather, who had always been with us before. We often spoke of him, because we missed him, or because he belonged to our stories, and we could not tell them without speaking of him.

One morning, perhaps to acknowledge to herself that he would not wear them again, my grandmother gave me a pair of my grandfather's shoes.

It was a gift not easy to accept. I said, "Thanks, Granny," and put them under my arm.

"No," she said. "Put them on. See if they fit."

They fit, and I started, embarrassedly, to take them off.

"No," she said. "Wear them."

And so I wore them to the field.

"New shoes!" Burley said, recognizing them, and I saw tears start to his eyes.

"Yes," I said.

Burley studied them, and then me. And then he smiled and put his arm around me, making the truth plain and bearable to us both: "You can wear 'em, honey. But you can't fill 'em."

It got to be September, and the fall feeling came into the air. The days would get as hot as ever, but now when the sun got low the chill would come. It was not going to frost for a while yet, but we could feel it coming. It was the time of year, Elton said, when a man begins to remember his long underwear.

We were cutting a patch at Elton's place where the rows were longer than any we had cut before, bending around the shoulder of a ridge and rising a little over it. They were rows to break a man's heart, for, shaped as they were, you could not see the end, and those of us who were strung out behind the leaders could not see each other. All that we could see ahead of us would be the cloudless blue sky. Each row was a long, lonely journey that, somewhere in the middle, in our weariness, we believed would never end.

Once when I had cut my row and was walking back to start another, Art Rowanberry wiped the sweat from his nose on the cuff of his sleeve and called out cheerfully to me, "Well, have you been across? Have you seen the other side?"

That became the ceremony of that day and the next. When one of us younger ones finished a row and came walking back, Art would ask us, "Have you seen the other side?"

Burley would take it up then, mourning and mocking: "Have you reached the other shore, dear brother? Have you seen that distant land?" And he would sing,

> Oh, pilgrim, have you seen that distant land?

On the evening of the second day we had the field nearly cut. There was just enough of the crop left standing to make an easy job of finishing up—something to look forward to. We had finished cutting for the day and were sitting in the rich, still light under a walnut tree at the edge of the field, resting a little, before loading the wagons. We would load them the last thing every evening, to unload the next morning while the dew was on.

We saw my father's car easing back along the fencerow, rocking a little over the rough spots in the ground. It was a gray car, all dusty, and scratched along the sides where he had driven it through the weeds and briars. He still had on his suit and tie.

"Ah, here he comes," Burley said, for we were used to seeing him at that time of day, when he would leave his office at Hargrave and drive up to help us a little or to see how we had got along.

He drove up beside us and stopped, and killed the engine. But he did not look at us. He looked straight ahead as if he had not quit driving, his hands still on the wheel.

"Boys," he said, "Mr. Feltner died this afternoon. About an hour ago."

And then, after he seemed to have finished, he said as though to himself, "And now that's over."

I heard Burley clear his throat, but nobody said anything. We sat in the cooling light in my grandfather's new silence, letting it come upon us.

And then the silence shifted and became our own. Nobody spoke. Nobody yet knew what to say. We did not know what we were going to do. We were, I finally realized, waiting on Jarrat. It was Elton's farm, but Jarrat was now the oldest man, and we were waiting on him.

He must have felt it too, for he stood, and stood still, looking at us, and then turned away from us toward the wagons.

"Let's load 'em up."

The
Wild
Birds
(1967)

"Where have they gone?" Wheeler thinks. But he knows. Gone to the cities, forever or for the day. Gone to the shopping center. Gone to the golf course. Gone to the grave.

He can remember Saturday afternoons when you could hardly find space in Hargrave to hitch a horse, and later ones when an automobile could not move through the crowd on Front Street as fast as a man could walk.

Wheeler is standing at his office window, whose lower pane announces Wheeler Catlett & Son, Attorneys-at-Law; he is looking out diagonally across the courthouse square and the roofs of the stores along Front Street at the shining reach of the Ohio, where a white towboat is shoving an island of coal barges against the current, its screws roiling the water in a long fan behind it. The barges are empty, coming up from the power plant at Jefferson, whose dark plume of smoke Wheeler can also see, stretching out eastward, upriver, under the gray sky.

Below him, the square and the streets around it are deserted. Even the loafers are gone from the courthouse where, the offices shut, they are barred from the weekday diversions of the public interest, and it is too cold to sit on the benches under the Social Security trees, now leafless, in the yard. The stores are shut also, for whatever shoppers may be at large are out at La Belle Riviere Shopping Plaza, which has lately overborne a farm in the bottomland back of town. Only a few automobiles stand widely dispersed around the square, nosed to the curbs, Wheeler's own and half a dozen more, to suggest the presence, somewhere, of living human beings— others like himself, Wheeler supposes, here because here is where they have usually been on Saturday afternoon.

But he knows too that he is *signifying* something by being here, as if here is where he agreed to be when he took his law school diploma and came home, or as near home as he could get and still practice law, forty-one years ago. He is here as if to prove "to all to whom these presents may come" his willingness to be here.

And yet if he is here by agreement, he is here also in fidelity to what is gone: the old-time Saturday to which the country people once deferred all their business, when his old clients, most of them now dead, would climb the stairs to his office as often as not for no business at all, but to sit and speak in deference to their mutual trust, reassuring both to them and to him. For along with the strictly business or legal clientele such as any lawyer anywhere might have had, Wheeler started out with a clientele that he may be said to have inherited—farmers mostly, friends of his father and his father-in-law, kinsmen, kinsmen's friends, with whom he thought of himself as a lawyer as little as they thought of themselves as clients. Between them and himself the technical connection was swallowed up in friendship, in mutual regard and loyalty. Such men, like as not, would not need a dime's worth of legal assistance between the settling of their parents' estates and the writing of their own wills, and not again after that. Wheeler served them as their defender against the law itself, before which they were ciphers, and so felt themselves—and he could do this only as their friend.

"What do I have to do about that, Wheeler?" they would ask, handing him a document or a letter.

And he would tell them. Or he would say, "Leave it here. I'll see to it."

"What I owe you, Wheeler?"

And he would name a figure sometimes to protect himself against the presumptuousness and long-windedness of some of them, or to protect the pride of others. Or he would say, "Nothing," deeming the work already repaid by "other good and valuable considerations."

So Wheeler is here by prior agreement and pursuant history— survivor, so far, of all that the agreement has led to. The office has changed little over the years, less by far than the town and the country around it. It contains an embankment of file cabinets, a small safe, a large desk, Wheeler's swivel chair, and a few more chairs, some more comfortable than others. The top of the desk is covered with books and file folders neatly stacked. On the blotter in the center is a ruled yellow tablet on which Wheeler has been writing, the top page nearly covered with his impatient blue script. By way of decoration, there are only a few photographs of Wheeler's children and grandchildren. Though the room is dim, he has not turned on a light.

A more compliant, less idealistic man than Wheeler might have been happier here than he has been, for this has been a place necessarily where people have revealed their greed, arrogance, meanness, cowardice, and sometimes their inviolable stupidity. And yet, though he has known these things, Wheeler has not believed in them. In loyalty to his clients, or to their Maker, in whose image he has supposed them made, he has believed in their generosity, goodness, courage, and intelligence. Mere fact has never been enough for him. He has pled and reasoned, cajoled, bullied, and preached, pushing events always toward a better end than he knew they could reach, resisting always the disappointment that he knew he should expect, and when the disappointment has come, as it too often has, never settling for it in his own heart or looking upon it as a conclusion.

Wheeler has been sketching at a speech. In that restless hand of his, that fairly pounces on each word as it comes to him, he has refined his understanding of the points to be made and has worked out the connections. What he was struggling to make clear is the process by which unbridled economic forces draw life, wealth, and intelligence off the farms and out of the country towns and set them into conflict with their sources. Farm produce leaves the farm to nourish an economy that has thrived by the ruin of land. In this way, in the terms of Wheeler's speech, *price* wars against *value*.

"Thus," he wrote, "to increase the *price* of their industrial products, they depress the *value* of goods—a process not indefinitely extendable," and his hand rose from the page and hovered over it, the pen aimed at the end of his sentence like a dart. The last phrase had something in it, maybe, but it would not do. At that failure, his mind abruptly refused the page. A fidelity older than his fidelity to word and page began to work on him. He picked up another pad on which he had drawn with a ruler the design of a shed to be built onto his feed barn. The new shed would require changes in the dimensions of the barn lot and in the positions of two gates, and those changes he had drawn out also. His mind, like a boy let out of school, returned to those things with relief, with elation. His thoughts leapt from his speech to its sources in place and memory, the generations of his kin and kind.

For the barn is the work of Wheeler's father, Marcellus, who built it to replace an older barn on the same spot. So methodical and clever a carpenter was Marcellus that he built the new barn while the old one stood, incorporating the old into the new, his mules never absent a night from their stalls, and he did virtually all the work alone. The building of the barn was one of the crests of the life of Marce Catlett, a pride and a comfort to him to the end of his days. Adding a new shed to it now is not something that Wheeler can afford to intend lightly or do badly.

Why at his age—when most of his generation are in retirement, and many are in the grave—he should be planning a new shed is a question he has entertained dutifully and answered perhaps a trifle belligerently: Because he *wants* to.

But his mind had begun a movement that would not stop yet. His mind's movement, characteristically, was homeward. What he hungered for was the place itself. He saw that his afternoon's work in the office was over, and that was when he got up and went to the window, as if to set eyesight and mind free of the room. He would go soon. By going so early, he would have time to salt his cattle.

This sudden shift of his attention is so familiar to him as almost to have been expected, for in its fundamental structure, its loyalties and preoccupations, Wheeler's mind has changed as little in forty years as his office. If change happens, it happens; Wheeler can recognize a change when he sees one, but change is not on his program. Difference is. His business, indoors and out, has been the making of differences. And not the least of these has been this shift that he is about to make again from office to farm.

But for a moment longer he allows himself to be held at the window by the almost solemn stillness of the square and the business streets of the little town, considering again the increasing number of empty buildings, the empty spaces where buildings have been burned or torn down and not replaced, hating again the hopeless expenditure of its decay.

And now, directly across from his office door, a pickup truck eases in to the curb; two men and a woman get out. Wheeler recognizes his cousin, Burley Coulter, Burley's nephew Nathan, and Hannah, Nathan's wife. The three come together at the rear of the truck, the woman between the two men, and start across the street.

"What are *they* doing here?" Wheeler wonders. And then from their direction he understands that they have come to see him. He smiles, glad of it, and presently he hears their footsteps on the stairs.

The footsteps ascend slowly, for Burley is past seventy now and, though still vigorous, no longer nimble.

Wheeler goes through the outer office, where his secretary's typewriter sits hooded on its desk, and meets them in the dim hallway at the top of the stairs, reaching his hand to them as they come up.

"Hello, Hannah. Go right on in there in the office, honey. How're you, Nathan? Hello, Burley."

"How you making it, Wheeler?" Burley says in his hearty way, as if speaking to him perhaps across a wide creek. "I told them you'd be here."

"You were right," Wheeler says, glad to feel his presence justified by that expectation. It is as though he has been waiting for them.

Burley's hand is hard and dry, its grip quick on his own. And then Wheeler lays his hand on the shoulder of the older man, pressing him toward the door, and follows him through into the greater light of the windowed rooms.

In his office he positions chairs for them in a close arc facing his chair. "Sit down. I'm glad to see you."

They take chairs and he returns to his own. He *is* glad to see them, and yet seeing them here, where they regard him with a certain un-accustomed deference, is awkward for him. He sees them often, Burley and Nathan especially, but rarely indoors, and today they have made a formal occasion of their visit by dressing up. Hannah is wearing a gray suit, and looks lovely in it, not to Wheeler's surprise, for she is still a beautiful woman, her beauty now less what she has than what she is. Nathan is wearing a plaid shirt, slacks, and a suede jacket. Burley, true to custom, has put on his newest work clothes, tan pants and shirt, starched and ironed to creases stiff as wire, the shirt buttoned at the throat but without a tie, a dark, coarse wool sweater, which he has now unbuttoned, and he holds on his lap, as delicately as if it is made of eggshell, his Sunday hat. Only the hat looks the worse for wear, but any hat of Burley's will look the worse for wear two hours after he has put it on; the delicacy of his hold on it now, Wheeler knows, is a formality that will not last, a sign of his uneasiness within his own sense of the place and the occasion. In his square-cut, blunt hand, so demanding or quieting upon hound or mule or the shoulder of another man, he holds the hat so that it touches without weight the creased cloth of his pants.

"Kind of dreary out, Wheeler," he says.

"Yes. It is, Burley. Or it looks dreary since it clouded up. I haven't been out. I was *going* out, though, pretty soon."

"Well, we won't keep you very long."

But Wheeler didn't mean to be hinting, and to make up for it, though he knows they have come on business, he says, "You're caught up in your work, I reckon."

Nathan laughs and shakes his head. "No."

"None of us, these times, will live to be caught up," Burley says. "We finished gathering corn yesterday. Monday morning, I reckon, we'll take a load of calves to the market. After that we'll be in the stripping room."

But Burley is waiting, Wheeler sees, for permission to begin his business. "Well," he says, "what have you got on your mind?"

"Wheeler," Burley says, "I want you to write my will."

"You do?" Wheeler is surprised and embarrassed. One does not normally write a person's will point-blank in the presence of his heirs. For Burley to bequeath his farm to Nathan right under Nathan's nose strikes Wheeler as a public intimacy of a sort. He is amazed to hear himself ask, "What for?"

"Well, Wheeler, I'm old enough to die, ain't I?"

Wheeler grins. "You always have been." He leans back in his chair as if to make the occasion more ordinary than he can feel it becoming. "Well then, Nathan, you and Hannah should probably let Burley and me talk this over alone."

"But Hannah and Nathan ain't in it, Wheeler. They ain't going to be in it."

Wheeler sits up. He says, "Oh," though that is not what he meant to say. And then, deliberately, he says, "Then who is in it?"

"Danny Branch."

"Danny." Though he was determined not to be, Wheeler is again surprised. The springs of his chair sing as he leans slowly back. For a long moment he and Burley sit and look at each other, Burley smiling, Wheeler frowning and staring as if Burley is surrounded by a mist.

"Danny? You're going to leave your half of your daddy's place, Dave Coulter's place, old George Coulter's place, to Danny Branch?"

"That's right."

"Why?"

"He's my boy, Wheeler. My son."

"Who said he is?"

"Well, Wheeler, for one, I did. I just said it."

"Do you have any proof?"

Burley has not perceptibly moved, but his thumb and middle finger, which at first pinched just the brim of his hat, have now worked their way to the base of the crown, the brim rolled in his hand. "I ain't *looking* for proof, Wheeler. Don't want any. It's done too late for proof. If there's a mistake in this, it has been my life, or a whole lot of it."

"Did Kate Helen say he was yours?"

Burley shakes his head, not going to answer that one. "Now Wheeler, I know you know the talk that has said he was my boy, my son, ever since he was born."

Wheeler does know it. He has known it all along. But it is irregular knowledge, irregularly known. He does not want to know it, or to admit that he knows it. "Talk's talk," he says. "Talk will be talk. To hell with talk. What we're dealing with now is the future of a good farm and the family that belongs to it, or ought to."

"Yes indeed."

"I don't think you ought to take a step like this, Burley, until you know for sure."

"I know all I want to know, more than I need to know."

Wheeler says, "*Well . . . ,*" ready to say that *he*, anyhow, can think of several questions he would like to know the answers to, but Burley raises the hand with the hat in it and stops him.

"It finally don't have anything to do with anything, Wheeler, except just honesty. If he's my boy, I've got to treat him like he is."

"But you do treat him like he is, and you have. You gave him half his upbringing, or three-quarters. Right up to Kate Helen's death you saw that he raised a crop and went to school and had what he needed. You've taken him to live with you, him and Lyda and their children, and you've . . ." Wheeler stops, realizing that he is saying nothing that all four of them do not already know.

"But now it's time to go beyond all that. Now I have to say that what belongs to me will belong to him, so he can belong to what I belong to. If he's my boy, I owe that to him free and clear."

"Suppose he's not."

"Suppose he is."

Wheeler is slouched low in his chair now, in the attitude, nearly, of a man asleep, except that his fingers are splayed out stiffly where they hang over the ends of his chair arms, and his eyes are widened, set on Burley in a look that would scour off rust. It is not a look easily met.

But Burley is looking back at him, still smiling, confidently and just a little indulgently smiling, having thought beyond where they have got to so far.

"It's wayward, Wheeler. I knowed you'd say what you've said. Or anyhow think it. I know it seems wayward to you. But wayward is the way it is. And always has been. The way a place in this world is passed on in time is not regular nor plain, Wheeler. It goes pretty close to accidental. But how else *could* it go? A deed nor a will, no writing at all, can tell you much about it. Even when it looks regular and plain, you know that somewhere it has been chancy, and just slipped by. All I see that I'm certain of is that it has got to be turned loose—loose is the way it is—to who knows what. I can say in a will, and I'm going to, that I leave it to Danny, but I don't know how it's going to him, if it will, or past him, or what it's coming to, or what will come to it. I'm just the one whose time has come to turn it loose."

Now it seems that they are no longer looking at each other, but at a cloud between them, a difference, that they have never before come so close to making or admitting. Whatever there may have been of lawyer and client in this conversation is long gone now, and Wheeler feels and regrets that departure, for he knows that something dark and unwieldy has impinged upon them, that they will not get past except by going through.

It is Burley's word *wayward* that names the difference that they are going to have to reckon with. Wheeler's mind makes one final, despairing swerve toward the field where his cattle are grazing. For a moment he sees it as he knows it will look now in the wind of late November, in the gray light under the swift clouds. And then he lets it go.

Wayward—a word that Burley says easily. If the things of this world are wayward, then he will say so, and love them as they are. But as his friends all know, it is hard to be a friend of Wheeler's and settle for things as they are. You will be lucky if he will let you settle for the possible, the faults of which he can tell you. The wayward is possible, but there must be a better way than wayward. Wheeler can remember Burley's grandfather, George Washington Coulter. He wrote his father's, Dave Coulter's, will here in this very room. He does not remember not knowing Burley, whom he has accompanied as younger kinsman, onlooker, and friend through all his transformations, from the wildness of his young years, through his years of devotion in kinship and friendship, to his succession as presiding elder of a company of friends that includes Wheeler himself.

It has a pattern clear enough, that life, and yet, as Wheeler has long known without exactly admitting, it is a clear pattern that includes the unclear, the wayward. The wayward and the dark.

Almost as suddenly as his mind abandons its vision of the daylit field, Wheeler recalls Burley as a night hunter. Back in his own boyhood and young manhood, he used to go hunting with Burley, and so he knows the utter simplicity of Burley's entrances into the woods.

He gets out of his car at the yard gate and walks across the dark yard and back porch to the kitchen door, to find Burley waiting for him. "*Here* you are! I was about to go ahead."

Burley is at the door, ready to go, his Smith and Wesson twenty-two in its shoulder holster, hat and coat already on. He pulls on his overshoes, takes his lantern from its nail and lights it, steps off the porch, calls the dogs, and walks down over the brow of the hill. Within two hundred steps they are enclosed in the woods along the river bluff, the damp of the night cold on their faces. Along that margin of steep wild ground between the ridges and the gentler slopes lower down, where the woods has stood unmolested from before memory, they walk in the swaying room of yellow lantern light, their huge tapering shadows leaping from tree to tree beside them. And soon, from off in the dark, beyond time, the voice of a hound opens.

It was another world they went to. Wheeler, as often as he went, always went as a stranger and a guest. Or so it seemed to him, as it seemed to him that Burley went always as a native, his entrance into the wild darkness always a homecoming.

One night when they have made a fire and sat down to wait while the dogs make sense of a cold trail, Burley goes to sleep, lying on his back on a pile of rocks, the driest bed available, and wakes an hour later, intently listening. "Dinah's treed. Let's go."

Sometimes Nathan would be with them or Nathan's brother, Tom, before he went to the war and was killed, or, rarely, Old Jack Beechum or, later, Elton Penn, and nearly always the brothers, Martin and Arthur Rowanberry.

On a moonless, starless night, late, in the quiet after a kill, the dogs lying on the leaves around them, they realize that they are lost. Intent upon a course flagged through the dark by the hounds' cries, they have neglected the landmarks. Now they stand around the lanterns under a beech in a little draw on a steep, wooded hillside, debating which way they may have come. Below them they can hear water running, but they cannot be sure in which branch.

"Naw," Arthur Rowanberry says to his brother, "we come by that little barn on the Merchant place and down through the locust thicket."

"Yes, and *then* we went up the Stillhouse Run, that's what we all know, but how many hollers did we pass before we turned up this one?"

"Well, I don't know."

That is what it keeps coming back to and they all laugh. The debate is being conducted partly for pleasure, for they are not *much* lost, but they are tired now and would rather not risk finding themselves by going in the wrong direction.

Finally Burley, who has said nothing, but has stood outside the light, looking and thinking, says, "*I* know where we are."

And they all turn to him.

"Where?"

"Where?"

"Right here."

Though Wheeler is now long past any yen he ever had to roam the woods at night, he knows that Burley is still a hunter, and, with Danny Branch and the Rowanberrys, still a breeder of hounds. At Burley's house at this moment, probably asleep in their stall in the barn, there is a bluetick hound named Rock, another older one named Sputnik, and a bitch by the name of Queen. And now Wheeler's older son, Andy is apt to be in the company of the hunters on the thawing or the rainy winter nights, and that is the way Wheeler has learned some of the things he knows.

He knows, he has always known, that as often as he has hunted with companions, Burley has hunted alone. The thought of Burley solitary in the woods at night has beguiled Wheeler's imagination and held it, more strongly perhaps than anything else outside the reach of his own life. For he knows—or from his own memory and from hearsay he is able to infer—that at those times Burley has passed over into a freedom that is old and, because it is strenuous and solitary, also rare. Those solitary hunts of his have always begun by chance or impulse. He may be out of the house already when they begin—on his way afoot to visit a neighbor after supper, maybe, followed by the dogs, who pick up a trail, and he is off. Or he will wake in the night, hearing his dogs treed away on the bluff below his house or in a thicketed slue hollow in the river bottom, and he will get up and go to them, leaving the warm bed, and so begin a route through the dark that may not bring him home again until the sun is up. Or the fever, as he calls it, will hit him while he is eating supper, and he will go, pausing only to strap on the pistol, light the lantern, and stick into the game pocket of his canvas hunting coat an apple or two, a handful of cold biscuits, perhaps a half-pint "against the chill." They start almost accidentally, these hunts, and they proceed according to the ways of coon and hound, or if the hunting is slow, according to the curiosity of a night traveler over his dark-estranged homeland. If he goes past their house, he may call to the Rowanberrys to join him or at least turn loose their dogs. If he sees a light still on in the river bank cabin of his friend, the retired barber, the fisherman, Jayber Crow, who will be up reading by the fire, he may go in and visit or, if it is late and turning cold, spend the night. In his young manhood, before responsibilities began to call him home, these solitary hunts might carry him away two days and nights, across long stretches of the country and back again, ignoring the roads except to cross them, not seen by a human eye, as though in the dark traverses of his own silence he walked again the country as it was before Finley and the Boones, at home in it time out of time.

He has been a man of two loves, not always compatible: of the dark woods, and of the daylit membership of kin and friends and households that has cohered in one of its lineages through nearly a century of living memory, and surely longer, around Ben Feltner, and then Jack Beechum, and then Mat Feltner, and then Burley's brother, Jarrat, and now around himself. So Wheeler has known him. But it has made him more complex than Wheeler knows, or knows yet, that double love. He has never learned anything until he has had to—as he willingly says, as perhaps is so—but he has had to learn a good deal.

For Wheeler, behind this neatly, somewhat uncomfortably dressed Burley Coulter here in his office, there stands another and yet another: the Burley of the barns and fields of all their lives and of his own loyally kept place and household, and then the Burley of the nighttime woods and the wayward ways through the dark.

In Wheeler's mind the symbol of Burley's readiness to take to the woods at nightfall is the tan canvas hunting coat—or, he must suppose, the succession of them, though he does not remember ever seeing Burley in a new one—that he has worn through all the winters that Wheeler has known him, on all occasions except funerals, tobacco or livestock sales, or trips to Hargrave on business, such as this. The coat, as Wheeler remembers it, is always so worn that it seems more a creature than an artifact, ripped, frazzled, crudely patched, short a button or two, black at the edges. As a farmer, Burley seems, or has come to seem, constant enough, and yet, even as such, to Wheeler he has something of the aspect of a visitor from the dark and the wild—human, friendly to humans, but apt to disappear into the woods.

If Burley has walked the marginal daylight of their world, crossing often between the open fields and the dark woods, faithful to the wayward routes that alone can join them, Wheeler's fidelity has been given to the human homesteads and neighborhoods and the known ways that preserve them. Through dark time and bad history, he has been keeper of the names that bear hope of light to the human clearings, and an orderly handing down. He is a preserver and defender of the dead, the more so, the more passionately so, as his acquaintance among the dead has increased, and as he has better understood the dangers to their living heirs. How, as a man of law, could he have been otherwise, or less? How, thinking of his own children and grandchildren, could he not insist on an orderly passage of these frail human parcels through time?

It is not as though he is unacquainted with the wayward. He has, God knows, spent his life trying to straighten it out. The wayward is a possible way—because, for lack of a better, it has had to be. But a better way is thinkable, is imaginable, and Wheeler, against all evidence and all odds, is an advocate of the better way. To plead the possibility of the merely possible, losing in the process all right to insist on the desirability of what would be better, is finally to lose even the possible—or so, in one way or another, Wheeler has argued time and again, and against opponents of larger repute than Burley Coulter. If he is set now to do battle with his friend, his purpose is not entirely self-defense, though it is that.

He does not forget—it has been a long time since he has been able to forget—that he is making his stand in the middle of a dying town in the midst of a wasting country, from which many have departed and much has been sent away, a land wasting and dying for want of the human names and knowledge that could give it life. It has been a comfort to Wheeler to think that the Coulter place, past Burley's death, would live on under that name, belonging first to Nathan, whom Wheeler loves as he loves Burley, and then to Nathan's son, Mattie, Matthew Burley Coulter. That is what he longs for, that passing on of the land, in the clear, from love to love, and it is in grief for that loss that he is opposing Burley. But this grief has touched and waked up the larger one, and the old anger that goes with it. How many times in the last twenty years has Wheeler risen to speak, to realize that the speech he has prepared is a defense of the dead and the absent, and he is pleading with strangers for a hope that, he is afraid, has no chance?

"It was wayward when it come to me," Burley is saying. "Looked like to me I was there, born there and not someplace else, just by accident. I never took to it by nature the way Jarrat did, the way Nathan here, I think, has. I just turned up here, take it or leave it. I might have gone somewhere else when I got mustered out in 1919, but I come back, and looked like I was in the habit of staying, so I stayed. I thought of leaving, but the times was hard and Pap needed me—or needed somebody better, to tell the truth—and I stayed. And then Pap died and Mam was old, and I stayed on with her. And when she died I stayed on and done my part with Jarrat; the boys was gone then, and he needed me. And somehow or other along the way, I began to stay because I wanted to. I wanted to be with Jarrat, and Nathan and Hannah here, and Mat and you and the others. And somewhere or other I realized that being here was the life I had because I'd never had another one any place else, and never would have.

"And that was all right, and is, and is going to be. But it looks like a bunch of intentions made out of accidents. I think of a night now, Wheeler—I lie awake. I've thought this over and over, from one end to the other, and I can't see that the way it has been is in line with what anybody planned or the way anybody thought it ought to be."

"But they did plan. They hoped. They started hoping and planning as soon as they got here—way back yonder."

"It missed. Or they did. Partly, they were planning and hoping about what they'd just finished stealing from the ones who had it before, and were already quarreling over themselves. You know it. And partly they were wrong. How could they be right about what hadn't happened? And partly it was wayward."

"But what if they *hadn't* planned and hoped—the ones that did anyhow—the good ones."

"Then we wouldn't know how far it missed, or how far we did, or *what* we missed. I ain't disowning them old ones, Wheeler."

"But now it's your time to plan and hope and carry it on. That we missed doesn't make any difference."

"No. That time's gone for me now, and I've missed probably as bad as the worst of the others. Now it's my time to turn it loose. You're talking to an old man, Wheeler, damn it!"

"Well, you're talking to an old man too, damn it, but I've still got some plans and hopes! I still know what would be best for my place!"

"I know the same as you, Wheeler. I know what would be best for my place too—somebody to live on it and care about it and do the work. And I know what it would look like if somebody did. But I come here today to turn it loose. And I've got good reason to do it."

"You've got a better reason than you've told me?"

Burley has been sitting upright on his chair as if it were a stool. Now he sags back, and for a moment sits staring at Wheeler without paying any particular attention to him, as if he doesn't notice or it doesn't matter that Wheeler is staring back at him. And then he says, "Cleanse thou me from secret faults."

"*What*?"

"Cleanse thou me from secret faults." As always when he quotes Scripture, Burley is grinning, unwilling, as Wheeler knows, to be entirely serious about any part of it that he can understand, even though, once he has understood it, he may be entirely willing to act on it.

Recognizing the passage now, Wheeler grins too, and then laughs and says what otherwise he would not say, "Well, Burley, mighty few of *your* faults have been secret."

And that is pretty much a fact. Burley Coulter's faults have been public entertainment in the town and neighborhood of Port William ever since he was a boy, most of his transgressions having been committed flagrantly in the public eye, and those that were not, if they had any conceivable public interest, having been duly recounted to the public by Burley Coulter himself. His escapades have now, by retelling, worn themselves as deeply into that countryside as its backroads.

Wheeler himself has loved to tell the story of Burley's exit from the back door of Grover Gibbs's house, having paid his compliments to Beulah Gibbs, as Grover returned unexpectedly through the front door. Carrying his clothes in his arms through a night black as the inside of a gourd, Burley ran through the stock pond behind the barn, and then, heading downhill into the woods, got behind a big calf who was going slower than he was, whereupon, according to him, he cried, "Calf, get out of the way! Let somebody run that knows how!"

"All that's past," Wheeler says. "Whatever was wrong in it can be forgiven in the regular way. When the psalmist said 'thou,' he didn't mean anybody in Port William or Hargrave. That account's not to be settled here."

"But some of it is." Burley's smile is now gone altogether. "Listen, Wheeler. I didn't come to take up a lot of your time, but we've done got this started now. I'm not telling you what you need to know to be my lawyer. I'm telling you what you need to know to be my friend. If a lawyer was all I wanted, I reckon I wouldn't have to hire a friend."

"You're not hiring a friend. You *have* one. Go on."

"Well, Kate Helen was an accommodating woman, too accommodating some would say, but she was good to me, Wheeler. We had what passed with me then for some good times. When I look back at them now, they still pass with me for good, though they come up with more results than I expected. I ain't going to go back on them, or on her, though I'm sorry, Lord knows, for some of the results."

There is a tenderness in Burley's voice now that Wheeler did not expect, that confesses more than he is yet prepared to understand, but it gives Kate Helen a standing, a presence, there in the room, one among them now, who will not lightly be dismissed. And Wheeler is carried back to a day in his own life when he passed along the creek road in front of Kate Helen's house, and saw her sitting on the porch in a rocking chair, barefooted, a guitar forgotten on her lap, a red ribbon in her hair. He has never forgotten. And the Kate Helen who attends them now, in Wheeler's mind as perhaps in Burley's, is Kate

Helen as she was then—a woman, as Burley used to say, who could take up a lot of room in a man's mind. In Wheeler's opposition to Burley there is no uncertainty as to what Burley saw when he looked at Kate Helen; Wheeler saw too, and he remembers. But now she has come back to him with something added to her: all that was said or implied in the gentleness with which Burley spoke of her. If she is with them now, Burley is now with them as her protector, and there are some things that Wheeler might have said about her that he is not going to say, and will never say again. He feels under his breastbone the first pain of a change.

But he turns to Nathan. "Is this what you want? If it wasn't to be Danny Branch's, it would be yours—your children's." He is holding out against what he sees he will have to give in to, still determinedly doubting what he knows he is going to have to believe, and his voice has the edge of challenge in it. He will not settle easily for the truth just because it happens to be the truth. He wants a truth he can like, and they are not surprised.

As his way is, Nathan has been sitting without moving, staring down at the toe of his shoe, as if he is shy perhaps, and now he makes only the small movement that brings his gaze up to meet Wheeler's. It is the look of a man utterly resolved to mean what he says, and Wheeler feels the force of it.

"I know what Uncle Burley wants, Wheeler, and it's all right. And I aim to stick to Danny."

Burley passes his hand through the air, the hat still in it, but forgotten now; it is just along for the ride. "I've not asked that of him, Wheeler. I don't ask anything. If Nathan sticks to Danny after I'm dead, that'll be fine, but my ghost won't trouble him if he don't."

Wheeler turns to look at Hannah, knowing what to expect, but his eyes tax her nevertheless, making it difficult.

"Yes," she says, nodding once and smiling at him, being as nice to him as she can be, though he can sense how much she is forbearing. "It's what we all want. It's best." And without looking away from Wheeler, she reaches for Burley's left hand, and drawing it over into her lap holds it in both of her own. To Wheeler's surprise then, her eyes suddenly fill with tears.

And then his own do. He looks down at his hands. "Well."

"Wheeler," Burley says, "Nathan and Hannah are going to have enough land, and their children too—"

"What if they weren't?"

"—and Danny's a good boy, a good young man."

"What if he wasn't?"

"There's no use in coming with them what-ifs, Wheeler. I ain't responsible for them. They dried up and blowed away long years ago. What if I had been a better man?

"If Nathan needed what I've got, I'd have to think of that. He don't. Besides what he has got on his own, he's his daddy's heir, and in the right way. You might say that he has come, as far as he has got anyhow, by the main road, the way you have, Wheeler, and has been regular. I haven't been regular. I've come by a kind of back path—through the woods, you might say, and along the bluffs. Whatever I've come to, I've mostly got there too late, and mostly by surprise.

"I don't say everybody *has* to be regular. Being out of regular may be all right—I liked it mostly. It may be in your nature. Maybe it's even useful in a way. But it finally gets to be a question of what you can recommend. I never recommended to Jarrat's boys or Danny or your boys that they ought to be careless with anything, or get limber-legged and lay out all night in a hayrick. Your way has been different from mine, but by my way I've come here where you are, and now I've got to know it and act like it. I know you can't make the irregular regular, but when you have rambled out of sight, you have to come back into the clear and show yourself."

"Wait now," Wheeler says. "I didn't—"

But Burley raises his hand and silences him. It is as if they recognize only now a change that has been established for some time: Burley has quietly, without gesture, assumed the role of the oldest man—the first time he has ever done this with Wheeler—and has begun to speak for Wheeler's sake as well as his own.

"I know how you think it ought to be, Wheeler. I think the same as you. I even thought once that the way things ought to be was pretty much the way they were. I thought things would go on here always the way they had been. The old ones would die when their time came, and the young ones would learn and come on. And the crops would be put out and got in, and the stock looked after, and things took care of. I thought, even, that the longer it went on the better it would get. People would learn; they would see what had been done wrong, and they would make it right.

"And then, about the end of the last war, I reckon, I seen it go wayward. Probably it had been wayward all along. But it got more wayward then, and I seen it then. They began to go and not come back—or a lot more did than had before. And now look at how many are gone—the old ones dead and gone that won't ever be replaced, the mold they were made in done throwed away, and the young ones dead in wars or killed in damned automobiles, or gone off to college and made too smart ever to come back, or gone off to easy money and bright lights and ain't going to work in the sun ever again if they can help it. I see them come back here to funerals—people who belong here, or did once, looking down into coffins at people they don't have anything left in common with except a name. They come from another world. They might as well come from that outer space the governments are wanting to get to now.

"When I think of a night, Wheeler, my mind sometimes slants off into that outer space, and I'm sorry the ones that knowed about it ever brought it up—all them lonesome stars and things up there so far apart. And they tell about these little atoms and the other little pieces that things are made out of, all whirling and jiggling around and not touching, as if a man could reach his hand right through himself. I know they know those things to blow them up.

"I lay my hand on me and quiet me down. And I say to myself that all that separateness, outside and inside, that don't matter. It's not here and not there. Then I think of all the good people I've known, not as good as they could have been, much less ought to have been, none of them, but good for the good that was in them along with the rest—Mam and Pap and Old Jack, and Aunt Dorie and Uncle Marce, and Mat and Mrs. Feltner, and Jarrat and Tom and Kate Helen, all of them dead, and you three here and the others still living. And I think of this country around here, not purely good either, but good enough for us, better than we deserve. And I think of what I've done here, all of it, all I'm glad I did, and all I wish had been done different or better, but wasn't."

"You're saying you're sorry for what you've done wrong? And by what you're proposing to do now you hope to make it right?"

"No! God damn it, Wheeler—excuse me, Hannah—no! What is done is done forever. I know that. I'm saying that the ones who have been here have been the way they were, and the ones of us who are here now are the way we are and to *know* that is the only chance we've got, dead and living, to be here together. I ain't saying we don't have to know what we ought to have been and ought to be, but we oughtn't to let that stand between us. That ain't the way we are. The way we are, we are members of each other. All of us. Everything. The difference ain't in who is a member and who is not, but in who knows it and who don't. What has been here, not what ought to have been, is what I have to claim. I have to be what I've been, and own up to it, no secret faults. Because before long I'm going to have to look the Old Marster in the face, and when He says, 'Burley Coulter?' I hope to say 'Yes, Sir. Such as I am, that's me.'"

And now he leans forward and, the hat brim rolled and clenched in the outer three fingers of his right hand, hooks his forefinger into the breast pocket of Wheeler's vest. He does not pull, but only holds, as gently as possible given the hand's forthrightness and the rigor in the crook of the old finger.

"And, Wheeler, one thing I am is the man who cared about Kate Helen Branch—all her life, you might say."

"You loved her," Wheeler says.

"That's right."

"You were a husband to her—in all but name."

"That's right."

"And you're her widower—in all but name."

"That's right."

Burley unhooks his finger and leans back. He is smiling again.

And finally the direction of this meeting declares itself to Wheeler. What Burley is performing, asking him to assist in, too late but none the less necessarily, is a kind of wedding between himself and Kate Helen Branch. It is the secrecy of that all-but-marriage of his that has been his great fault, for its secrecy prevented its being taken seriously, perhaps even by himself, and denied it a proper standing in the world.

"And so that secret fault you've been talking about—that didn't have anything to do with the things we've all always known."

"No."

"It was secret love."

"That's right. In a way I don't think I even knowed it myself, Wheeler. Anyhow, not for a long time. Not till too late."

Wheeler is smiling too now, asking and listening, helping him along. "Why didn't you clear all this up any sooner?"

"I've never learned anything until I had to, Wheeler. That's the kind of head I've got."

"And you've been learning this a long time?"

"Years and years. Pret' near all my life I've been figuring out where I am and what I'm responsible for—and, as I said, pret' near always too slow and too late. Some things haven't got my attention until they knocked me in the head."

"But you and Kate Helen were involved in this friendly connection for a long time. She must not have minded."

"That had a lot to do with it. We *were* friends, and she *didn't* mind—or didn't seem to."

Burley crosses his arms over his lap, going ahead now on his own.

"You remember the little paper-sided house in Thad Spellman's thicket field that she and her mother moved into after her daddy died—there by the creek road at the foot of the hill. I could get there from town you might say by gravity, and at first that was usually how I got there.

"This is how it went. I want you to know.

"On Saturday night I'd walk to Port William and loaf around in one place and another a few hours, visiting, maybe shoot a game or two of pool. And after while I'd get me a pint from Alice Whodat and stroll out across the ridge, drinking along the way, listening to the sounds and looking all around at whatever there was light enough to see—free as a bird, as they say, and, as far as I can remember, nothing on my mind at all. Sometimes if the night was warm and dry, I'd sit down somewhere and sing a while. None of the real things that have happened to me had happened then. My head might as well have been a cabbage, except I could eat and drink with it. And after while I'd tumble down through the woods and the bushes to Kate Helen's house.

"And maybe the first real thing that ever happened to me was that I started going down there because I *liked* to. I liked Kate Helen. I liked to sit and jaw with old Mrs. Branch. Sometimes I would go there in broad daylight, just to visit, if you know what I mean, and we would sit and talk and laugh. Part of it, I guess, was what you said. Kate Helen didn't mind. Or up to a point she didn't, however far that was. She liked me and her mother did too. And they wasn't *at* me all the time—which for a while I thought was pretty low class of them, I will admit.

"They were poor, of course, which anybody could see, and so it come about that whenever I went there I would gather up a few groceries, things I knew they needed, and bring them along, or if we'd killed hogs I'd bring a middling or a sack or two of sausage. And I'd always try to save out a head or two for them. The old woman was a great one to make souse, and made the best too that ever I ate. And then I got so I'd help them make a garden. And then in the winter I took to getting up their firewood. They needed those things to be done, and I was the only soul they had to do them. I liked being of use to them better than anything.

"But oftentimes, I'd go there just to sit a while and visit. We'd talk or listen to the radio, maybe pop some corn. Sometimes we'd play and sing a little."

Wheeler might never have remembered it again. He had forgot that he remembered. But now in thought he comes again down through the steep fields along the side of the little creek valley. He is hunting, supposedly, his shotgun lying in the crook of his arm, and busily quartering the slope ahead of him is his good English setter by the name of Romney; but the weather is dry, they have found no birds, and, submitting to the charm of the warm, bright, still afternoon, he has ceased to pay attention to the dog. He has idled down along the fall of the valley, pausing to look, watching the little fields and the patches of woodland open ahead of him with the intense, pleased curiosity that idleness on such an afternoon can sometimes allow. And now, climbing over a rock fence at the edge of a strip of woodland into a pasture, he pauses again, and hears in the distance a few muted, dispersed notes that it takes him a minute or two to recognize as human singing.

The curve of the slope presently brings him around to where he can see the square of tin roof within the square of yard and garden within the close network of leafless thicket overgrowing Thad Spellman's abandoned field. And now the voices are carried clearly up to him, rising and braiding themselves together over the sweet pacing of a fiddle and guitar:

> Oh, he taught me to love him and called me his flower,
> A blossom to cheer him through life's dreary hour,
> But now he has gone and left me alone,
> The wildflowers to weep, the wild birds to mourn.

Wheeler knows who they are. Burley he has heard play before at a dance or two, a little embarrassedly "filling a gap" in a band, and has even heard him sing, though only emblematic scraps of songs sung out raucously at work. Now he realizes that Burley is better at both than he thought, though in both playing and singing his manner is straightforward and declarative, almost a speaking in support of the melody, which is carried by Kate Helen. It is Kate Helen's voice that takes Wheeler by surprise—by a kind of shock, in fact; he expected nothing like it—for it is so strongly clear, so feelingly precise.

They finish the song and laugh at the end of it and speak a little, words that he cannot hear, and begin another—and another and another. The dog finally comes back and lies down at Wheeler's feet, and still he stands and listens—until it comes to him that they play and sing so well because they believe that nobody is listening. He turns away then, embarrassed for himself, and makes his way back up the long hollow onto the upland and to his father's place again, the country remaining bemused around him in the hovering late warmth and light, and the two voices seeming to stay with him a long part of the way, as if they too hung and hovered in the air:

I'll dance and I'll sing and my heart shall be gay. . . .

"My lord," he thinks, "that was forty years ago!"

It was forty years ago almost to the day, he thinks, and remembering the intelligent clarity of that voice lifted into the bright air that carried it away, he says, "And Kate Helen never did say anything? Never did suggest maybe that you two ought to get married?"

"Fact is, she never did. And you'll wonder why, Wheeler, and I can't tell you. I could give you some guesses, I've thought about it enough. But as for knowing, I don't. I don't know, and won't ever."

"She thought you were a lucky catch any way she could get you," Hannah says to him, patting his hand. It is something Wheeler can tell that she has said to him before. And then she says, more seriously, "She thought you were better than she deserved. So did her mother, I'll bet."

"Well, I wasn't. But whatever her reason was, not to know it is wrong. It's the very thing that's wrong."

They pause at that failure, allowing it its being. And then Burley speaks on, describing his long odd-times domestic companionship with Kate Helen. He tells of Danny's birth: "I purely did not think of that ahead of time, Wheeler. It was a plumb surprise. And yet it tickled me." He tells of the death of old Mrs. Branch; and of how, as Danny grew, time and usage grew on him and Kate Helen; how he depended on her and was dependable, took her and was taken for granted, liking the world too well as it was, "laying aside wars and such," to think how it might be improved, usually, until after his chance to improve it had gone by; how in time she became sick and died; how at her death, seeing it all then, he would have liked to have been openly and formally her mourner, but, faithful to appearances, he had shown himself only an interested bystander, acting a great deal more like himself than he felt. Behind appearances, he paid the doctor, paid the hospital, paid the undertaker, bought a lot in the cemetery; saw to everything—as Wheeler knew pretty well at the time, and attributed to guilt of conscience—as quietly as he has done for the others who have been his declared dependents.

Danny, grown by then, was still living with his mother at the time of her death.

"You just as well come on, now," Burley said, "and live with me." For then he saw it the way it should have been—though he let Danny go on calling him "Uncle Burley," as he acknowledges now to Wheeler, and is shaken once by a silent laugh.

"Well, now that Mammy's gone, I want to get married."

"Well, bring the gal. I got a big house."

As though he has now finally lived in his own life up to that time when Danny came to live with Burley, Wheeler admits him into his mind. Or, anyhow, Danny Branch now turns up in Wheeler's mind, admitted or not, put there by the words of his would-be lawful father, after the failure of all events so far to put him there, and his face now takes its place among the faces that belong there.

Danny, Wheeler would bet, is not as smart as Burley, but he does look like him in a way; he has Burley's way of looking at you and grinning and nodding his head once before saying what he has to say—a fact that Wheeler now allows to underwrite Burley's supposition and his intent. He allows Burley's argument to make sense—not all the sense there is, but enough.

And so with Wheeler's consent Danny comes into their membership and also is one there with them, Wheeler already supposing that Nathan will not be the only one who will stick to Danny, and looking forward to the possibility of his own usefulness to that young man.

As often, the defeat of his better judgment has left him only with a job to do, a job that he *can* do, and he feels a sudden infusion of good humor. If Danny is Burley's son and heir, and if that is less than might have been hoped, it is what they are left with, what they have, and Wheeler will be as glad as the rest of them to make the most of it.

He feels preparing in himself the friendship for Danny Branch that these three, after all, have come to ask him for—and which, all three know, probably better than Wheeler, will be a gift and a blessing to the younger man, and also undoubtedly something of a burden, for once Wheeler has Danny on his mind he will be full of advice for him that Danny will not easily ignore.

As soon as he has a chance, Wheeler thinks, he will stop by for a visit with Burley and Danny and Lyda and the little ones. He would like, for one thing, to see if there is any resemblance to Burley or the other Coulters showing up in Danny's children.

"*So,*" he says. "You just want to leave everything to Danny. That won't take but a few words. I'll get it typed up first thing Monday morning, and you can come in and sign it." He smiles at Hannah and Nathan. "You all can come with him and be witnesses."

He leans back in his chair, having, as he thinks, brought the meeting to an end. He is ready for them to go, ready to go himself. He allows the wind and the gray sky back into mind.

Burley is busy restoring the shape of his hat, as though he might be about to put it on, but he does not. He looks up at Wheeler again and studies him a moment before he speaks.

"Wheeler, do you know why we've been friends?"

"I've thought so," Wheeler says. He has thought so because of that company of friends to which they both belong, which has been so largely the pleasure and meaning of both their lives. "But why?"

"Because we ain't brothers."

"What are you talking about?" Wheeler says.

But he is afraid he knows, and his discomfort is apparent to them all. Nathan and Hannah obviously feel it too, and are as surprised as he is.

"If we'd been brothers, you wouldn't have put up with me. Or anyhow you partly wouldn't have, because a lot of my doings haven't been your kind of doings. As it was, they could be tolerable or even funny to you because they wasn't done close enough to you to matter. You could laugh."

Wheeler sits forward now, comfortless, straight up in his chair, openly bearing the difficulty he knows it is useless to hide. Though this has never occurred to him before, because nobody has said it to him before, he knows with a seizure of conviction that Burley is right. He knows they all know, and again under his breastbone he feels the pain of a change that he thought completed, but is not completed yet. A great cavity has opened at the heart of a friendship, a membership, that not only they here in the office and the others who are living but men and women now dead belong to, going far back, dear as life. Dearer. It is a cavity larger than all they know, a cavity that somebody—their silence so testifies—is going to have to step into, or all will be lost.

If things were going slower, if he had the presence of mind he had even a minute ago, Wheeler would pray for the strength to step into it, for the *knowledge* to step into it. As it is, he does not know how. He sits as if paralyzed in his loss, without a word to his name, as if suddenly pushed stark naked into a courtroom, history and attainment stripped from him, become as a little child.

But Burley is smiling, and not with the vengeful pleasure that Wheeler feared, but with understanding. He knows that what he has given Wheeler is pain, his to give, but Wheeler's own. He sees.

"Wheeler, if we're going to get this will made out, not to mention all else we've got to do while there's breath in us, I think you've got to forgive me as if I was a brother to you." He laughs, asserting for the last time the seniority now indisputably his, and casting it aside. "And I reckon I've got to forgive you for taking so long to do it."

He has spoken out of that cavity, out of that dark abyss.

It is as if some deep dividing valley has been stepped across. There can be no further tarrying, no turning back. To Wheeler, it seems that all their lives have begun again—lives dead, living, yet to be. As if feeling himself simply carried forward by that change, for another moment yet he does not move.

And then he reaches out and grips Burley's shoulder, recognizing almost by surprise, with relief, the familiar flesh and bone. "Burley, it's all right."

And Burley lays his own hand on Wheeler's shoulder. "Thank you, Wheeler. Shore it is."

Wheeler's vision is obscured by a lens of quivering light. When it steadies and clears, his sight has changed. Now, it seems to him, he is looking through or past his idea of Burley, and can *see* him at last, the fine, clear, calm, generous, amused eyes looking back at him out of the old face.

And Hannah, smiling again too, though she has averted her eyes, is digging in her purse for her handkerchief. "Well!" she says.

The office is crowded now with all that they have loved, the living remembered, the dead brought back to mind, and a gentle, forceless light seems to have come with them. There in the plain, penumbral old room, that light gathers the four of them into its shadowless embrace. For a time without speaking they sit together in it.

Wheeler stands looking down into the street over the top of the reversed painted legend: WHEELER CATLETT & SON, ATTORNEYS-AT-LAW. The day remains as it was, the intensity of the clouded light the same. Except that the towboat is gone now, the world seems hardly to have moved, the smoke from the power plant still tainting the sky.

In a little while Wheeler will leave the office and leave town. The room he stands in is driven out of his mind by the thought of the raw, free wind over the open fields. But he does not go yet. He thinks of the fields, how all we know of them lies over them, taking their shape, for a little while, like a fall of snow.

He watches Burley and Hannah and Nathan walk back to their truck, waiting for their departure to complete itself before he will begin his own.

Design by David Bullen
Typeset in Mergenthaler Sabon
by Harrington-Young
Printed by Maple-Vail
on acid-free paper

JM

F   Berry, Wendell
BER
          The wild birds

$8.95

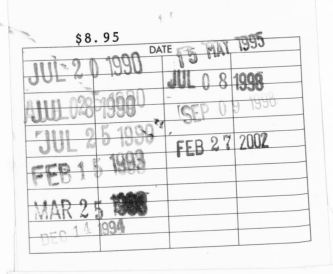

DATE		
JUL 20 1990		15 MAY 1995
		JUL 0 8 1998
JUL 02 1990		SEP 0 9 1998
JUL 25 1990		FEB 27 2002
FEB 15 1993		
MAR 25 1993		
DEC 14 1994		